I took the wallet out of the box. My hands were shaking. I knew there was more money in that wallet than I'd ever seen before, but I didn't know how much. I spread it open and without taking the money out, flipped through the bills one at a time. There were two fifties, a twenty, three tens, and four singles — a hundred and fifty-four dollars altogether. . . . Oh, it was a lot of money; it scared me, but it thrilled me, too. I could do a lot of things with that much money. I could buy Sally her dress, and me a new baseball glove; but mainly, it could keep the family from getting split up, for a while at least.

But taking the money would be stealing, and I didn't know that I had the nerve to do it. Would I do it?

". . . this is honest and affecting. . . . A melancholy riff that's in tune with universal feelings of responsibility and guilt. . . ."

—**Kirkus Reviews**

"The portrait of a floundering family is absorbing; Jack's character is well developed. . . ."

—**Booklist**

Give Dad My Best

by
James Lincoln Collier

Vagabond Books

SCHOLASTIC BOOK SERVICES
New York Toronto London Auckland Sydney Tokyo

ISBN 0-590-32634-1

12 11 10 9 8 7 6 5 4 3 2 1   6   2 3 4 5 6 7/8

For Kristin, Kate, Adam, and Miranda

1

fter dinner Sally went over to Margene Sheckley's, and the baby went outside to bounce his ball on the cellar door. Dad took his trombone out to the kitchen and unpacked it. I followed him out. "I haven't washed it for weeks," he said. "I never used to let it go this long."

"Dad," I said, "Sally needs a new outfit."

He rubbed his mustache. "I thought she had a lot of clothes," he said. Dad is sort of roly-poly and has a little mustache. Because of his round belly his shirt is always coming out of his pants.

"They're all worn out," I said.

"They can't be all worn out, Jack. Clothes all don't wear out at once."

"Well they are though," I said. "Besides, they're too small for her."

"I haven't noticed that. Why didn't she say something about it?"

"She didn't want to bother you over the money," I said.

He looked grumpy. "We're not that broke," he said.

I didn't say anything. He picked up the trombone bell, carried it over to the sink, and began washing it carefully with soap and water. "If you don't wash it, the metal gets pitted," he said.

"Sally would be pretty happy to have a new outfit before her play."

"All right," he said. "I'll get her one. How much does a new outfit cost?"

"About five dollars for the skirt and four for the jacket."

He didn't say anything. Then he said, "I heard they're going to reopen the country club any day now. Everyone says that business is starting to pick up."

Dad is always saying that something is going to happen any day now. "Did they promise it would?"

"I heard it on good authority, Jack. Any day now, they said. They promised me I could have the band again when they reopen. I'll easily clear fifty a week with tips. Maybe seventy-five. Even more maybe. Why I've seen weeks when we cleared a hundred or a hundred and a quarter, with tips."

"That was before the depression," I said. "That was back in 1929 before the stock market crashed."

"No it wasn't, Jack. That was as late as '31, '32. Besides, how would you remember? You were hardly born then."

"I was five during the crash. I can remember." I could too. There was just me and Sally. The baby hadn't been born yet. We lived in a big house up on

Lake Street with a huge backyard — well, I guess maybe it wasn't so huge, but it seemed huge to me, being so little. We had a swing thing with a trapeze on it, and a seesaw, that Dad suddenly brought back with him once when he came off the road. And Mom had a cleaning lady to come in, and she was always giving parties — afternoon parties like Mah-Jongg parties, of course, because Dad was on the road a lot and working most nights when he was home. Another time I can remember him coming off the road with his pockets stuffed with money and taking it out in handfuls and flinging it up into the air like dead leaves. Then the Crash came and we moved out of the house into a little apartment over a jewelry store on Main Street.

"You can't remember much of it," he said.

"I can remember the house on Lake Street."

"It was a nice house," he said. "I never gave a damn about things like that, but it pleased your mother. We had a lot of money then. I don't know where it all came from; it just seemed to keep coming in. I had more jobs than I could take; I could pick and choose. I'll be back up there again, too, one of these days. Once the country club reopens. The band business is coming back. Look at Tommy Dorsey. A few years ago he was scuffling like the rest of us and now he's rolling in dough. Heck, I can play that sweet style; there isn't anything to that. And then I could get a book together — write a few special arrangements myself and use stocks to fill out the book until I got going and could buy some originals. It's all in the sound — having a distinctive sound of your own, the way Miller voices the clarinet over the saxes. It's just a matter of getting that

3

sound, and once you have that the big agencies come flocking around and you're off and running."

Back before the Crash we had plenty of money. Dad was hardly ever out of work in those days. He worked with Mal Hallett a lot, who was one of the big bands up here in Massachusetts. He played in pit bands in Boston sometimes and he substituted with the Boston Symphony a few times and once he even played with the Jean Goldkette band, which had the great Bix Beiderbecke in it, when they came through Worcester and one of the trombone players was sick. Most of the time, though, he played club dates — weddings and parties and the regular dances at the country club. "I could have gone with Whiteman," he always told people, "but that meant being on the road all the time, and I had a family." He even made some records with a band he had with a friend of his. It was called Dave Warren's Jolly Lads, Dave being his friend's name and Warren being his. He always said, "The records were catching on when radio came in and killed the record business." He had a lot of bad luck like that. He figured he would have done a lot better if it hadn't been for bad luck, like the depression. He boasted a lot about how good a trombone player he was, which I wished he wouldn't do. But I guess it was true. He could play swing or sweet; he could read and he could improvise. "That's why Whiteman wanted me to come on the band so badly. A lot of those jazz players he had couldn't read for shoot. But I had a family and your mother didn't want me to go on the road. I'd have been sitting pretty if I'd done it. Once you've played with Whiteman your name gets known. There was plenty of work around home so I stayed, and by the time the depression came and there wasn't any work anymore, it was too late to go with Whiteman. It was just my bad luck."

"Listen, Dad," I said. "So I can tell Sally it's okay about the outfit?"

He got down a kitchen towel and began drying off the bell of the trombone. "I'll speak to her about it."

"She needs it pretty soon."

"You let me worry about it, Jack."

It always made me nervous to talk to him about things like that. He hated it when you brought up money — he just never wanted to talk about it. "Listen, Dad, why don't you try to get a day job?"

"No," he said. "Forget about that."

"You did it once."

"I'll never do it again," he said. He put the bell back in the case and took out the slide.

I could remember that, too. It was when we were living in the apartment over the jewelry store on Main Street. I was in the second grade and I came home from school one day and some men were carrying all of our furniture down the stairs and putting it onto the sidewalk. Mom was crying and Dad was there with the landlord shouting and cursing. Oh, it made me feel sick to see my bed sitting on the sidewalk, still made up with sheets and blankets, only a little rumpled up from being carried down the stairs; and the dining-room table, too, with the chairs piled on top of it. It was so queer and I started to cry, but then Mom saw me and took me over to the neighbors. They gave me some custard pie and a bottle of Moxie and I stopped crying. After a while we went home. The furniture was all back where it belonged.

5

Dad explained to me that it had been a mistake, but the next day he got a job picking apples in an orchard near Stevenstown, and a while after that — I can't remember exactly when — we moved to this place. And a while after that Mom started to get crazy.

"Dad, maybe you could get a day job for just a little while." I hated opposing him like that.

"Don't even mention it, Jack. I'm no apple picker, I'm a musician. I don't work with my hands." He soaped up the slide.

"Even for a little while? I mean just until they reopen the country club."

He shook his head. "Jack, once you start in on a day job you never get out of it again. Look at Dave, he went into the cotton mill four years ago and he hasn't played since."

"Yes he has. You had that job over at — "

"All right, all right. He gets a few jobs. But he'll never get out of the mill."

"Just for a little while. Maybe Mom will get better soon."

He didn't even answer that.

"Dad, what would happen if we really went broke, I mean completely broke?"

He began to dry off the slide. "Oh, Jack, you worry too much. I always manage to come up with something, don't I? I've kept a roof over our heads and food on the table, haven't I?" As he finished wiping off the slide he began to sing, "Happy days are heeeeere again, the skies above are cleeeear again," which was the Democrats' theme song from the last election in 1936, when Roosevelt won. Dad thought Roosevelt was terrific. He let us stay up late

6

on election night and listen to the returns on the radio. He kept saying it was something we'd remember all our lives, listening to Roosevelt's great victory in 1936. We wouldn't remember it, though, because we all fell asleep before it was over. That was when we still had a radio. It broke last year and finally Dad sold it to somebody for a couple of bucks. He was planning to get a new one as soon as he got a few good gigs.

"The one I love is neeeeear again, Happy days are heeeeere again," he sang. He put the slide back in the case and snapped it shut. Then he came over, put his arm around my shoulder the way he always did, and gave me a squeeze. "Jack, you're just an old worrywart. It doesn't do any good. Try to look on the bright side — things have a way of working out." Then he put his hand in his trousers pocket, pulled out his change, and looked at it. There were two nickels and a dime lying in his palm. Just enough for four beers. "I'm going out for a walk," he said. "Make sure the baby is in bed by nine, and see that Sally does her homework." He took his hat down from the top of the icebox, where he always kept it, and left.

I went out into the living room and got the record player and put it on the kitchen table. I figured Sally would come home soon to do her homework and I didn't want to bother her with the music. I checked the needle, but it seemed okay, so I didn't change it. Dad was always big on changing the needles all the time, because he was afraid of ruining his records. He had a lot of records, all kinds of stuff, a lot of Whiteman and Goldkette, and some of the jazz bands like Ellington and Fletcher Henderson, and of

7

course some of the new swing stuff — Goodman and the Casa Loma Orchastra — but he had a lot of classical records, too, those twelve-inch Victor Red Seal sets that cost a lot of money. It made Mom furious when he would bring home new records, because we couldn't spare the money, but Dad always said that it was a business expense; it was like nails to a carpenter, he had to keep up with what was going on. And I guess he believed that; but the truth was that he was crazy about records and couldn't resist buying at least one whenever he was in the record store. I've seen him do it — take the record out of the rack and put it back, and take it out again. And then he'd shake his head and say, "Nope, I can't afford it this week." So he'd shove it back; but before he even got his hands off it, he'd snatch it out of the rack and say, "Well, it's a tax deduction," and reach in his pocket for the money.

So I had a lot of records to choose from. I thought about it for a minute, and then I took out Debussy's *Sunken Cathedral,* which was sort of spooky and sad. A lot of times when I was worried and didn't feel too hot, I liked to listen to it. I don't know why listening to a sad record when you're feeling down makes you feel better, but it does. At least it does to me. So I put on the *Sunken Cathedral* and sat there by the kitchen table listening to it and playing the parts I really liked over again.

I guess nobody knows why people go crazy, not even the doctors. At least nobody could figure out what was the matter with Mom. I guess living in our place didn't help very much. It was just a little place behind a grocery store, except the grocery store had gone out of business and was empty. The grocer used to live in our place and have his store out front. When he closed up we got the place for twenty-five dollars a month. It was pretty terrible. The linoleum on the kitchen floor was all cracks, so that pieces kept breaking off, and the paint was peeling from the ceilings, and the wallpaper had big stains in a couple of places where a pipe had leaked through the wall sometime. There were only two bedrooms, one for Mom and Dad and one for us kids. Of course all three of us couldn't fit into one bedroom, so usually I slept on the daybed in the living room. Or if Dad had a gig and was going to be out late, Sally would move in with Mom, and I'd take her bed, and Dad would sleep on the daybed when he got home. There wasn't any real heat in the place, either, just a kerosine heater in the kitchen and another one in the living room. In real cold weather you had to leave the bedroom doors open partway so they'd stay warm. But in the middle of winter the bedrooms never got very warm no matter what you did, so mostly Sally and I would have to our homework at the kitchen table, which is one reason why I stopped bothering to do it. How could you do your homework with somebody else right there jiggling around her chair and shaking the whole table when she erased something? There wasn't any yard, either, just an alley that came up beside the building and out back a cement parking place where they used to keep the garbage cans from the grocery store. It was okay for the baby to bounce his ball around in, but it wasn't much fun to sit there. Dad always said it was just temporary. I remember when we moved in, he went around being jolly and cheerful and saying look on the bright side, it was sort of like camping out;

we'd move soon when things got better. But after we'd been there two years Mom went crazy.

I don't guess too many people have their mothers go crazy, but it was pretty terrible. At first you sort of don't notice it — I mean you put it out of your mind. I remember when it first started, I'd come home from school and she'd be sitting in her bedroom on the side of the bed with no lights on, not doing anything, just sitting there with her fists sort of clenched up in her lap. I'd look at her and say, "Hi, Mom," as if she were normal, and go away, and after a few minutes she'd snap out of it and make dinner. But it was scary each time it happened — you had the feeling that she wasn't your mother anymore but some stranger. Naturally, after it was over you'd put it out of your mind and pretend it never happened.

But then she got worse, and we couldn't pretend anymore. For example, one time she was sitting there after dinner finishing her coffee. Dad was telling some musician story — he has a lot of funny musician stories — and suddenly Mom began pushing all the plates off the table onto the floor and Dad had to leap up and grab her. She began to scratch his face and they wrestled around, and she was crying and trying to get away. But finally he calmed her down and put her to bed and she went on crying for a long time afterwards. It scared us kids. We sat there frozen in our chairs, not able to move.

Another time Sally came home from school and there was Mom in the living room with a big pair of sewing scissors in her hand, all frenzied and crazy, trying to scratch the wallpaper off the wall. Sally ran out and got Dad out of the Colonial where he was having a beer, and he called the doctor. The doctor put her in the hospital, but she came home after a few days. We couldn't afford it, she said, and besides the nurses were doing dirty things with the doctors, and when she complained nobody would do anything about it.

Finally she began saying she wanted to go back home. Back home was down in New Orleans where my grandparents lived. I hardly knew them. We visited there once when I was very little, and a couple of times they came to visit us when we had the house on Lake Street. Dad said they didn't like him. They didn't like the idea that their daughter had married a musician. Dad met Mom when she was going to college at Mount Holyoke. He played some kind of dance there and somehow they met at the dance and started going together. Then Dad got an offer to go on the road with Art Hickman. They were going to California and Mom wanted to go, too, so she ran off with Dad and got married. She used to say, "We drove all the way to the Coast in this Reo Speedwagon your father had. At the time it seemed like a very romantic idea, to run off with a magician. The other girls were wild with envy when they heard about it." But my grandparents were in a rage. They blamed it all on Dad and they wouldn't speak to him for a while, but then when I was born they wanted to see their grandchild, so they forgave Dad a little and would come to visit us sometimes.

I don't know why Mom was so eager to go down there to see them; she had never wanted to visit them before. But suddenly it was all she could talk about. Dad didn't want her to go; I guess he was afraid she would never come back. But finally she insisted so much that Dad helped her pack and took her down to the train station, and she went. And about two months later we got a letter from my grandparents saying that she was in a mental home. They wouldn't tell us what had happened or anything. Naturally Dad went right down there — he had to borrow the money from Dave Johnson — and when he came back he said that Mom had lost her mind, it might be years before she was well, and she was better off down there because they had the money to look after her and we didn't.

It scared me a lot to think about my mother being crazy — to have somebody you know so well change into somebody different. It was sort of like getting messed up with bad magic. I used to lie in bed thinking about her, wondering what she was doing and how she was acting, and did she wonder about us and think of what we were doing? But to tell the truth, I was relieved not to have her around, and so were the other kids. I mean you didn't have to worry all the way home from school whether she'd be sitting in the dark when you got home, or stabbing at the wallpaper, or doing something else crazy. So we sort of reorganized the family, and a few weeks went by and we got used to it.

Sally came in. "Eeyah," she said.

"Where were you?" I said.

"None of your beeswax," she said. "How can I do my homework if you're playing records?"

"You can't hear in your room."

"Yes, I can. Besides, you're supposed to be doing your homework, too."

"You're not my boss," I said.

"You're not mine, either," she said.

"Who said I was?"

"Playing those records so loud."

"They're not loud," I said. "Besides, if you want to know, Dad told me to make sure you did your homework."

She didn't say anything, because she realized it was probably true. "I don't care. Where is he?"

"He went out for his usual walk."

"Oh," she said. "I want a glass of milk."

"You can't have any, there's just enough for breakfast."

She opened the icebox door and took out the milk bottle. It was about half full.

"Didn't believe me," I said. "If you drink that we'll have to eat our cornflakes with nothing on them."

"What am I going to drink?"

"Water," I said.

"Eeyah," she said. "Phooey. Has Dad got any money?"

"He's got the Elks Club gig tomorrow night. It's five dollars, and I'm supposed to work at Conklin's carrying groceries, so that's another dollar plus maybe a few tips. They're supposed to tip a dime but they don't always do it."

"Dad promised me would buy me a new outfit."

"What?" I said. "When did he promise that?"

"Just a little while ago. He was in the drugstore with Dave Johnson buying cigarettes."

I wished Dad wouldn't keep making promises like that. There were too many things that could go wrong. I mean last winter he had some gigs lined up and he promised the baby a sled, but then half the gigs fell through and he couldn't get the sled for

Henry. It wasn't Dad's fault for the gigs falling through, but the baby was pretty disappointed. "What were you doing in the drugstore?"

"Buying — none of your beeswax."

I figured she was probably buying lipstick with Margene Sheckley, but I didn't want to get into a fight about it. "Did he say when you could get your new outfit?"

"Before the play. He said he had a couple of good gigs coming up and I could get it before the play."

It made me sort of nervous to hear that. "Sometimes gigs fall through, Sal," I said. "I mean maybe they cancel the dance, or if it's a wedding they decide they can't afford a band after all. It isn't Dad's fault when it happens, it's just bad luck."

She stamped her foot. "I'm getting tired of being poor all the time. When is this damn depression going to be over?"

"I don't know," I said. "It doesn't seem to be getting over."

"Why doesn't Dad get a day job?"

"He's a musician," I said. "He shouldn't have to work with his hands."

"So what?" she said.

"So he's got a right to be a musician if he wants. Would you rather have a musician for a father or somebody who works in the mill?"

"Dave Johnson took a job in the mill."

I was getting mad. "Dad's better than Dave Johnson. Dad can play sweet or swing and he can read like a shot. He's too good for around here, they don't appreciate him. He ought to be with a big swing band."

"I don't care," Sally said. "I'm tired of being poor."

14

I was still mad. "Stop criticizing Dad all the time," I shouted. "He's doing the best he can, he's just had bad luck with the depression and all."

She knew I was mad. "I'm not *blaming* him, I just wish he'd get a day job."

The truth was, so did I. But I didn't say it.

She sat down and leaned on the table with her elbows. "We seem to be getting poorer and poorer," she said.

"It's hard to tell," I said. "If only Dad would tell us how much money he has, so we could figure it out. But he never will. If you want to know what I think, Sal, I think we're pretty broke."

She began to chew on her thumbnail.

"Don't do that," I said.

"You're not my boss, I can chew on my fingernails if I want."

"It'll give you blood poisoning," I said.

"Listen Jack, what happens if you're completely busted?"

"You have no money," I said.

"I know," she said, "but what happens?"

"I guess you go to live with somebody else. That's what happened to the Burtts. Eddie Burtt went out to New York State to work on his uncle's farm and Francie — I forget where Francie went."

"She went to Boston to live with her grandmother."

"Well, yeah," I said, "that's what happens."

She chewed on her fingernail for a minute and I was just about to tell her to stop when she said, "Well, where would we go?"

"We won't split up," I said.

"Yes, but if. . . ."

"We won't," I said.

"But if. . . ."

I thought about it. "I guess we'd go down to New Orleans to live with Grandpa and Grandma."

"We couldn't," she said. "They don't have enough room."

"Then we'd have to split up. Somebody would have to go to live in Chicago with Uncle Edgar and Aunt Mabel." Uncle Edgar was my mother's brother.

"I couldn't stand that," she said. Uncle Edgar and Aunt Mabel didn't have any kids. They were very strict. Sometimes we used to visit them; maybe if Dad was in Chicago on a job we'd all come out there and stay with them for a few days. They kept telling us to hold our fork right and sit up straight. It was pretty bad having somebody who wasn't your parent telling you stuff like that.

"Well, probably you'd get to go down to New Orleans to live with Grandpa. They like girls better."

"Jack, do you think it might happen?"

I wished we hadn't got into this discussion. "Dad's always come up with something. You're supposed to be doing your homework."

"You're not my boss."

"Dad told me to see that you did your homework."

"Are you going to do yours?" she said.

"None of your business," I said.

"I knew you weren't," she said. "You never do any homework. You'll probably flunk."

"Never," I said. "I'll never flunk. I'm too smart."

"I'm just as smart as you are."

"No you're not," I said.

"Yes I am," she said. She stuck out her tongue at me. "Phooey to you, and lots of them." Then she stomped off to do her homework, and I put the *Sunken Cathedral* back on again.

16

The thing about Dad is that, being a musician, he's different from most fathers. For example, one time I was sitting in school just after lunch and somebody came into the room and handed the teacher a note. She said, "Jack Lundquist, your father is down in the office." That seemed kind of funny, because Dad never paid any attention to our school. I should have figured he hardly knew where it was. When I got down to the office he was standing there and he said, "Let's go, Jack, we're late for your doctor's appointment."

I started to blurt out, "I don't have any — "

But quickly he put in, "Didn't Mom tell you, they changed it? Let's go." So we went outside and he began to laugh. There was a brand new Buick coupe sitting by the curb, all white and shiny, with the top down. "I've got a gig out in Springfield tonight. The leader lent it to me so I could bring the boys down. I figured as long as we have it we might as well drive up to Fenway Park and see the ball game."

I said, "Aren't you afraid that you might dent it?" But he wasn't, so we drove into Fenway and he bought me as many hot dogs and root beers as I wanted, and Jimmy Foxx hit two home runs, and the Red Sox won.

I could think of other things like that. Once he had a weekend gig at a fancy hotel down in New York. He took Sally and Mom down and put them up in the hotel and let Sally call down for room service any time she wanted for ice-cream sundaes and frappes and stuff. They spent up all the money he made on the gig, but he said it was worth it.

So he would do things like that sometimes. But other times he just seemed to forget all about us. He'd go off on the road for a couple of weeks and he

17

wouldn't call Mom up very often, and then he'd come back two days after he was supposed to and say, "Some of the boys figured that as long as we were in Chicago we ought to see the town a little." So it wasn't so much that he didn't want to do things for us; he was just sort of forgetful about us. And that was why it worried me when he promised Sally her outfit — by tomorrow he'd have forgotten all about it.

Sally came out into the kitchen. "I want something to drink," she said.

"You'll have to drink water if you're thirsty. I told you, there isn't any milk."

"Lend me a nickel," she said.

"All I've got is fifteen cents," I said.

"Well lend me a nickel of it."

"What happened to that fifty cents you had?"

She got red. "None of your beeswax."

That made me suspicious. "Well I can't help it if you waste your money on sodas."

"I didn't waste it on sodas," she said.

"Candy, then."

"Not candy, either."

"What, then?"

"It's none of your beeswax."

I decided not to start a fight about it. We didn't say anything. The music stopped, and I turned the record over and started to put the tone arm in the grooves. She grabbed my arm. "Don't play that. Tell me how we can stop being split up."

"Don't grab my arm like that, you might scratch the record."

"Help me think."

"Sal, stop worrying about it. Dad'll come up with something."

18

"Help me think."

"All right," I said, "I'll tell you a way. Get a million dollars."

"Be serious."

"Okay," I said. "If we could get some regular money coming in, we might be okay."

"How much?"

I thought about it. I wasn't really sure. I knew that Dave Johnson made around forty-five dollars a week working in the mill, because Dad had said so. The Johnsons had a nice house that they rented — not big, but not too old, and a car and a big radio and an electric refrigerator. "I guess if we had thirty-five dollars a week we would be okay."

"That isn't so much," she said.

"The heck it isn't," I said. "If I quit school and worked full time at Conklin's, all I could make — well, at twenty-five cents an hour it might come out to eleven or twelve dollars a week."

"Plus tips."

"Add on a couple of dollars for tips."

"Plus what Dad makes," she said.

"Look, he only worked nine nights in the past month, and four of them were those five-dollar jobs at the Elks Club."

"But that's regular."

"Sure, four Saturdays a month. And anyway, I can't quit school until I'm sixteen."

She didn't say anything, and neither did I. Then I said, "The only way we could get that much money is to steal it."

2

I'll admit it, I'd thought about stealing money
before. I don't guess I was the only one, either.
The depression got you to thinking that way.
I mean you might be walking down the street
and there in a bakery window would be a huge big
gooey chocolate éclair; and you'd be hungry anyway
from only having had one sandwich and a glass of
milk for lunch; and your mouth would start to water
and you could actually feel what the éclair would
taste like in your mouth. But it would cost a nickel,
and you couldn't waste a nickel on an éclair. Or
some friend of yours would have a terrific new
fielder's glove, all dark brown leather with a big
built-in pocket so you could hardly miss a grounder
even if you tried. All you'd have would be your old
glove with half the stuffing falling out, that you'd
bought from some kid for a dollar, and you'd go
around thinking about your friend's new glove all
day, trying to figure out a way to get five dollars for

20

one, too. But you knew that even if you got five dollars, you couldn't waste it on something like a baseball glove when you needed a new winter coat. Or, like, on the Fourth of July, some of the kids would have a whole bunch of firecrackers — cherry bombs and torpedoes and ash cans and stuff — and all you could afford was a couple of packages of ordinary firecrackers — well, those are the times that your mind might get onto the idea of stealing.

I had a daydream about it the next afternoon at Conklin's, where I worked sometimes. Conklin's was just an ordinary little grocery store. There was a counter down one side with a coffee grinder screwed down onto it, and a meat slicer, too, for cutting cold cuts out of the delicatessen case. You worked them by hand. They had come out with electric ones, but Mr. Conklin wouldn't buy them. "Anybody who's too lazy to turn a crank handle on a coffee machine can go work someplace else," he said. All the walls around the store were filled up with cans of soup and vegetables and bottles of soda and tomato juice and packages of soap and cereal and dried prunes and bags of flour and sugar and bread and all the other things you buy in a grocery store. Downstairs there was an old basement that smelled like dust and wet cement, where we stored the cases of food before they were unpacked. I spent a lot of my time down in that basement, unpacking stuff, sorting it out, or making inventories to see what we needed. It was pretty terrible down there, because there weren't any windows, and just one plain light bulb for light; it was kind of like being in a prison cell, especially on a nice day when I knew the sun was bright and warm outside and the air was fresh. It was much better when I could work upstairs at the counter, getting

21

the things down from the shelves as people asked for them, adding up the prices on a paper bag, and then packing the bag and carrying it out to the car, if the person came in one. Sometimes if there were a lot of bags to load in the car they'd tip me a nickel or even a dime. Old Man Conklin was pretty cheap. He paid me a dollar for working all day Saturday and fifty cents for working afternoons after school, which was only some of the time.

So when I'm working down in the basement unpacking cartons or sweeping up the store or washing the windows or something, I usually have a daydream so I can stand the boredom. My daydreams are usually about stealing, or being very powerful or even sometimes about killing. I admit, I'm kind of ashamed of my daydreams: I mean it isn't too good to daydream about killing or stealing all the time. If it's a night dream, you can't help what you dream about; but with a daydream you can choose, so you're sort of responsible for what you daydream about, and sometimes I feel guilty. But if I'm going to get really concentrated on a daydream it has to be something that interests me, and the things that interest me are pretty bad. Anyway, this day stealing was on my mind, and I figured I'd have a daydream about robbing somebody. I thought about who it might be, and I decided on Mr. Conklin:

I'm down in the basement with Mrs. Conklin doing an inventory and she says, "I have to go home and fix supper, Jack. You'll have to finish this up by yourself." She gets her purse from down off a shelf where she put it and goes up the stairs out of the basement. I wait a few minutes for her to go outside and get on her way home. Then I pick up the broom we keep down down there and take a baseball swing at the light bulb. It goes splat and the place is in total darkness. I fumble my way to the top of the stairs. Old Man Conklin is waiting on a customer. I stand there at the top of the stairs until the customer is gone. Then I say, "Mr. Conklin, the light bulb in the basement exploded." He says, "What, how could that happen?" I say, "I don't know, all of a sudden it just blew up. I was lucky I didn't get cut. I didn't want to mess with it." He sort of grumbles and gets a flashlight off the shelf under the counter. He says, "Watch the store, I'll be right up." Then he goes down the stairs into the basement. Quickly I turn to the register. I ease the No Sale key down slowly so the bell won't ring, and then I let the cash drawer slowly out. Quickly I snatch out the money. I jam it down into my pants and tuck it into the crotch of my underwear. Then suddenly I shout and knock a few cans off a shelf. I shout again, race to the front door and bang it a couple of times. Old Man Conklin comes charging up the stairs. He shouts, "What happened?" I shout, "Some big guy just ran in and swiped the money out of the cash drawer." He shouts, "What?" I "I was washing off the deli case, and he just ran in and grabbed the dough." Old Man Conklin stares at me. "You're lying, Jack, the deli case is dry. Where's the money?" I shout, "I didn't do it." He shouts, "Yes, you did. Take off your clothes." I shout, "No I won't." I grab up the carving knife lying on top of the deli case that we use for cutting cheese. I say menacingly, "Take one step nearer, Mr. Conklin, and I'll kill you."

But I'm sort of scared to kill him, even in my daydream. So I stood there unpacking cans of peeled tomatoes, trying to decide whether I ought to kill him, or how to end it, and then he shouted downstairs for me to bring up a case of Quaker Oats and I gave up the daydream.

Oh, I had a lot of these daydreams. There would never be more than fifty dollars or so in the cash register, but it wasn't fifty we needed. What we needed was a lot of money — a big pile of it — five hundred or a thousand dollars or something like that, which would keep us going for a while. And where could you steal that much money? It wasn't realistic.

I had other things to worry about, anyway. The biggest one was that the baseball season was starting, and how could I go out for the team if I was working at Conklin's after school? It was pretty important to me to make the team. I'd played shortstop on the junior high school team. I was the best fielder, which was why I played shortstop, and I could hit, too. I figured that I had a chance to make the high school varsity, even though most ninth-graders didn't make the varsity but played on the J.V. I didn't expect I would be a regular, but I figured I could make it as an infield sub — they usually had two infield subs on the team. The thing was, I wanted to make all-state by the time I was a junior at least. The reason for that was, I wanted to be a big league ballplayer when I grew up. I never told that to anybody — that would have seemed silly to them, some fourteen-year-old kid planning on getting into the majors. But somebody had to be major leaguers, why not me? What encouraged me about it was that about four years before, a guy from our high school almost got

24

into the majors. He was a catcher and he hit over .400 for three straight years. He was all-state and the Brooklyn Dodgers signed him for their farm when he graduated. He played for some team in Texas for a couple of years and then for Montreal. He was in the Dodgers' spring training camp twice and once, toward the end of the season, they brought him up for a couple of weeks. There were headlines in the Stevenstown newspaper about that. He got into a few games, but he didn't get any hits and after a while he fizzled out and you didn't see anything about him in the papers anymore.

But the thing was, it encouraged me that there wasn't anything crazy about somebody from a little town like this getting into the major leagues. Ballplayers had to come from somewhere. If this guy had got a couple of hits he might have made it. The Dodgers were one of the worst teams in the majors and they could use some good players. And how could I go out for the team if I was working at Conklin's after school? The extra five dollars a week was important. Besides, sometimes Old Man Conklin gave me left-over bread or rolls and stuff to take home.

The answer was to find a different kind of job. What I needed was some kind of job where I could work nights. Or maybe I could get a job in a dog wagon washing dishes, where I'd be able to start around five o'clock, after baseball practice was over. But getting any kind of a job was tough. I was lucky to have the one I had.

I was thinking about that when old man Conklin put his head down the cellarway and hollered, "Jack, come on up here. Be quick now." I was glad enough to be quick about getting out of that gloomy place, and I came on up. There was a guy there wearing a

25

captain's hat and white duck trousers. "Bring up six cases of beer and load them in Mr. Slater's station wagon out front."

"What kind of beer?"

"It doesn't matter," the man said. "Anything you've got." Only he didn't say "anything"; he said more like "eynathin'" — he had some kind of English accent.

"We've got plenty of Schlitz," I said.

"Schlitz it is, then. Somebody broke into the boat club last night and cleaned out the liquor supply, and the members will raise bloody 'ell if there's no beer for the weekend."

It didn't take me very long to load up the six cases of beer. I stacked them in the back of the station wagon, and then Mr. Slater came out with old man Conklin behind him. "Jack, drive up to the boat club with Mr. Slater and help him unload this."

"How am I going to get back?" I asked.

"You can walk — it's only three miles."

I didn't mind. Walking home on a nice day like that would be better than working down in the cellar of Conklin's store. "Okay," I said. I got into the station wagon, and we drove down Main Street and out through town to the lake. It turned out that Mr. Slater was a talker. He told me all about the robbery — the thieves had taken a couple of outboard engines and a lot of deck paint as well as the liquor. It was fun to listen to him talk in that English accent. He said "roight" for right, and "cayses of beer," and "ayle" for ale. "They didn't get into the sayfe," he said. "Likely there's a good sum in it, especially over the weekends when we cahn't get to the bienk."

"I didn't know you had dances at the boat club," I said.

"We didn't used to, but as the country club is shut up the members use it for private parties or wedding receptions sometimes."

"I guess you probably have to hire bands for the parties."

"I don't know about that. Whoever is arranging the party lays on the band. I'm just the steward."

Even though I'd lived in Stevenstown a long time I didn't know much about the boat club. It was for rich people. You had to have a lot of money to join it. It had been started a long time before, back in the nineteenth century, by people who had houses and summer places around the lake. Some of them were from Stevenstown, people like the Damsons who owned the cotton mill; but most of them were from Boston or even New York. The ones who didn't live too far away came down for weekends as soon as the weather was good in the spring. Then when school was out and it really got warm they'd come down and open up their houses. The rich people owned all the land around the lake. Somebody was always having the idea that the town ought to buy up some land on the lake so we could have a public swimming beach, but nothing ever came of it, especially now that we were in the depression. So the only way we could swim out there was to sneak in through somebody's property, which was kind of hard. But in winter, when the lake was frozen, we'd go down there and skate. It was terrific skating when you didn't have any snow. After it snowed, we'd clear the ice off, but it was always sort of rough then. And as you skated around you'd see the rich people's houses — some of them just sort of ordinary little places, but some of them almost like mansions. They all had docks, and most of them had boat houses right on the water. Sometimes we'd take off our skates and walk around the houses, trying to see inside. But mostly they were shuttered up, and you couldn't see anything. Sometimes kids would break into one of the houses and steal stuff or bust stuff up. But I never wanted to.

A lot of the men who belonged to the boat club were so rich, even during the depression they didn't have to work. They would come up for the whole summer and do nothing but sail their boats or fish or sit around and drink. I guess that drinking was one of the reasons why they started the boat club in the first place. The regular bars around Stevenstown were too low class for rich people; they needed to have a private bar where they could drink apart from the riffraff like us. It made me sore to think about rich people having so much money, and us having to struggle for it all the time. I wished I were rich, too.

There was a brick wall around the boat club with glass set into the top, so people couldn't climb over. You got in through the big iron gates. There was a sign over the gates in scrawly iron letters, which were hard to read, saying "Nipmuck Boating Association." Nipmuck was the name of the Indian tribe that used to live around Stevenstown before the whites came, but everybody just called it the boat club. We drove through the gates and down a long, winding, bluestone driveway. Being riffraff, I'd never been in the boat club before. There were big pine trees along the driveway. Through them I could see some tennis courts with people in white clothes flashing around on them. I'd never played tennis. To tell the truth, I'd never seen a tennis court close up.

Tennis was a rich people's game because it cost hundreds of dollars to put in a court and then you had to have fancy white clothes to play in. I wished I could try tennis. I figured I could learn it pretty quickly and beat the rich kids. I figured us riffraff were probably tougher and better athletes than rich kids.

The clubhouse was at the end of the driveway, about fifty feet from the shore of the lake. It wasn't very big. I was kind of disappointed. I had thought the clubhouse would be like one of those Southern mansions they have in the movies, but it was just a low white clapboard building with a big porch on the front facing the water. On the roof of the porch was a deck with a railing around it, where you could watch the sailboat races they had every Sunday. I knew about the races because they used to put them on the sports page of the paper. In front of the clubhouse at the edge of the water were three long docks sticking out into the lake. There were only a few boats tied up along the dock, because it was early in the season — mostly sailboats, but a few motorboats, too. Some people were messing around on the dock, working on their boats or getting ready to go out; there were a few boats already out, sailing along in the sunshine, with the water sparkling around them as they raced along. The breeze blew the smell of pines to us. Oh, it seemed so nice to be rich. Things were clean and neat and even the sunshine seemed to be brighter than down by our house, although I knew that couldn't be true. Sitting on the railing of the porch were a couple of kids my age. I figured they must be part of the Damson family. They were wearing bathing suits and clean white shirts and they were just lounging there with nothing to do but decide whether to go swimming or sailing or to play tennis. I hated them so; it wasn't fair.

Mr. Slater drove around to the rear of the clubhouse, opened up the back of the station wagon, and I started carrying the cases of beer inside. The clubhouse was mostly one big room with a fieldstone fireplace at one side. Along the front there was a row of windows looking across the porch out to the lake. In the back was a long bar. There was an elk's head over the bar, a huge stuffed swordfish over the fireplace, and lots of photographs of boats and races along the walls. Locked in a glass cabinet near the fireplace were a lot of silver trophies for tennis matches and sailing races. The rest of the room was empty except for some folded chairs along the walls and a few tables scattered around. Besides the big room there was a little office where Mr. Slater ran things, a couple of locker rooms with showers, and a storage room behind the bar. Mr. Slater showed me where to store the beer — some of it in the storage room, some of it in a big cooler behind the bar. I was loading up the cooler when the two kids in bathing suits came into the big room from the porch.

"Hey, Slater, how about giving us some cokes?" I was shocked to hear kids call a grown-up by his last name.

"You brats still 'aven't paid for the cokes you 'ad yesterday."

"Honest, we'll pay you as soon as my father gets here. He forgot to give me my allowance."

Mr. Slater looked at them. Then he said, "Jack, give 'em a couple of cokes out of the oice-box."

I turned away. I couldn't see Mr. Slater, but I knew he was standing there watching me and I knew what I was going to do. I got the cokes out, snapped off the caps with a bottle opener that was hanging from the bar sink by a string, and slid the bottles along the bar the way I'd seen the bartenders do at the country club when I'd gone there with Dad. Then I took a couple of glasses off the shelf by the sink and slid them down the bar, too.

"You ever work in a club, Jack?" Mr. Slater said.

I had my lie ready. "My father's a musician — sir. I used to help out up at the country club when he was working there, sometimes." The two kids were staring at me, too, and suddenly I realized that they were envying me, for being able to hang around bars and be a lot more grown-up than they were.

"I never saw you up there," Mr. Slater said.

"I didn't do it a lot," I said. "Just sometimes when Dad could fix it up."

The kids went on looking at me. "Is he working there now?"

I didn't say anything. Then I said, "There's still a couple of cases of beer in the station wagon, sir. I'll get them in."

I carried the last cases into the little storeroom and stacked them as neatly as I could in a corner. Then I went back out to the bar. "Mr. Slater," I said, "is there a broom around somewhere? There was a lot of dust on those cases and it got all over the back of your station wagon."

Mr. Slater stared at me, and then he said, "There should be one behind the storeroom door." I found it, went back out to the station wagon, and began sweeping out. There was hardly enough dust to see, much less sweep, but I kept brushing around as if there were a lot, and in about a minute, I realized that Mr. Slater was standing in the back door to the clubhouse, watching me.

I stopped sweeping and closed up the tailgate. "I guess that's got it," I said. I started to go back into the clubhouse to put the broom away, but he stopped me, the way I knew he would.

"Jack, what's your nayme?"

"Lundquist."

"Oh, roight, I know who your father is. Saxophone plier, in'it?"

"Trombone," I said.

"Oh roight, that's it. Used to 'ave the band at the country club quite a lot in the old days."

"He had most of the weekends for a long time, sir," I said. I didn't want to throw in too many *sirs*; it wouldn't sound right, but I figured a few wouldn't hurt.

"I could use a good kid out 'ere for a couple of days. I've got all this bloody insurance business to attend to due to the robbery. I could use somebody to do the cleaning up and run the bar at times. Are you required to work in that grocery store on Saturdays?"

"I don't work there regularly," I said. "Just sometimes."

"Know 'ow to mix a drink?"

I knew enough not to make my lie too big. "Well, not the fancy ones," I said.

He nodded. "I'll pay you a quarter an hour. Turn up at eight o'clock tomorrow morning and we'll see 'ow it goes."

My heart was pounding like a mallet on stone, because I knew that if I ever wanted to steal money, the best place to do it was where the rich people were.

3

When I got home, the baby was setting the table in the kitchen and Sally was stirring something in a big pot on the stove. Dad was in the bedroom playing warm-up exercises.

"You're late," Sally said. "How do you expect me to get dinner ready if people are always late?"

"I'm not always late," I said.

The baby thumped his spoon on the metal table-top. "We're hungry. Where've you been?"

The baby wasn't much of a baby. He was eight and he was pretty big for his age, bigger than most of the kids in his class. His real name was Henry. I didn't answer his question; I wanted to tell my story when everybody was together. "What's for supper?"

"Pea soup. I'm serving now. Go get Dad." She began getting down some bowls from the cabinet, and I went across the living room into Dad's bedroom. He had his Arban book out and was running mordants. Back in the old days he used to boast that he never warmed up, he'd just go down to the club, take his horn out of the case, and knock the job off. But nowadays he wasn't playing very much. His lip was out of shape and he liked to warm up for an hour before he went on the job.

"Supper's ready," I said.

"Sally's sore at you for being late."

"I was working."

We went out and sat down at the tin enamel table. We had only two real chairs for the kitchen table. When we'd moved out of the Lake Street house we'd had to sell the dining room set Dad had bought Mom after they got married. So all we had were these two wooden chairs, so the baby sat on the kitchen stool, and me and Sally argued over who had to sit on the rocker. Being late I took it because I didn't want to start an argument. Sally put down the bowls of pea soup and a loaf of bread. "That's all the butter there is," she said.

"Where's the milk?" the baby said.

"There isn't any milk," Sally said. "You'll have to drink water like the rest of us, Baby."

"Don't call me Baby."

"Henry."

"How can we be out of milk?" Dad said, rubbing his little mustache. "I just got two quarts yesterday."

"That was the day before, Dad," Sally said. "We use up more milk than that."

"I thought that was yesterday."

"No, it was Wednesday. I remember."

"All right, Sally," he said. "I'll give you some food money tomorrow."

I thumped the table with my spoon. "Guess where I was," I said.

"At Conklin's," the baby said.

"Wrong," I said. "You guess, Sally."

"I don't feel like guessing."

"Sally's mad at you for being late," Dad said.

"Why should I have to hang around here fixing dinner when Jack is out somewhere playing baseball?" she said.

"I wasn't playing baseball," I said. "If you want to know, I was out at the boat club."

"The boat club?"

"And I've got a job there."

It was pretty much fun to see how surprised they were. I was all the center of everything, and Sally got over being sore. So I told them all about it and how I figured on doing such a good job that Mr. Slater would take me on regularly; and maybe in the summer when they were really busy I could work it into a full-time job six or seven days a week and make fifteen or twenty dollars a week, especially if there were tips.

"Rich people don't tip," Dad said. "The people who tip is some ordinary guy when he goes out on a splurge once in a while. He tips because he thinks that's what rich people do. But the rich don't give big tips, because for them being out on a splurge is normal, they do it every day."

"Still, I bet they tip some."

"Oh sure, you'll get some tips," Dad said. "I can remember back before the depression, sometimes guys would tip us a hundred dollars to play requests. Once in Chicago some big gangster came into a place where I was playing and gave the leader five

35

hundred bucks to play 'Margie' all night long. Nothing but 'Margie.' See, his girl friend was named Margie and he was trying to impress her. Boy, we were sick of 'Margie' before the night was over, but there wasn't anything we could do about it, this gangster was pretty tough."

"What's the boat club like, Jack?" Sally said. She was pretty excited about the whole thing. She kept asking a lot of questions about what kind of clothes the people at the club wore and what they talked about. I knew that she was trying to find out what rich people were like and whether they were really the way they were in the movies, and I was pretty sure that sooner or later she'd start badgering me to take her out there, maybe get her a job there, too. And she'd end up making a big daydream about some rich kid falling in love with her and taking her to nightclubs and for rides in his car, the way it was in the movies. But she didn't want to come right out and say that she was curious about what it was like to be rich. In America the rich weren't supposed to be better than anybody else, and to be curious about them was sort of admitting that they were better.

So finally she changed the subject around so she could have something to talk about. "I've been trying to decide what color outfit to buy."

I took a quick look at Dad. "I don't know if we can afford a new dress yet," I said. How was he going to buy her a new dress if he couldn't afford a bottle of milk?

"Oh, we can afford it, Jack," Dad said. "Don't worry about it. If it's important to Sally, we'll manage somehow."

"I need it a week from next Wednesday," Sally said. "I need it before the play."

"Don't worry about it, Sally," Dad said. "I'll work out something." Then he said, "Listen Jack, you don't know anything about bartending. Let's go over to Dave Johnson's and have him show you a few tricks." A lot of musicians knew something about bartending because of the amount of time they spent in clubs, and I knew that Dave had actually worked as a bartender from time to time, when playing jobs were slack. But the truth was, Dad didn't care so much about Dave teaching me anything — it was just an excuse to have some fun. I didn't mind, though. I kind of liked going out with Dad and Dave and feeling like I was a man with them, too.

So Dad got his hat from the top of the icebox and we went out. Sally was sort of sore that she got left at home to look after Henry, but I didn't care, it was my night to be the star; she could be the star some other time.

The Johnsons lived about a mile away down at the end of Main Street toward the lake. It took us about fifteen minutes to walk there. Dave was down in the basement with his kid, Sven, who was about eight. Dave had a little shop down there — a lathe and a jigsaw and a bench saw and various sanders and stuff. He made outdoor furniture in his spare time — picnic tables and benches and Adirondack chairs and so forth. He made them in the winter and stored them in his backyard under a big piece of canvas; and in the spring and summer he sold them. Dave Johnson was a tall, thin guy, kind of stooped over. He had a big, droopy mustache, like a sheriff's in a *Saturday Evening Post* story, and he and Dad looked pretty funny up on the bandstand side by side — Dad all roly-poly with his little mustache and Dave Johnson tall and thin with his droopy mustache.

37

We went down into the basement and sat around on the benches and piles of lumber. "Sven, run up to the icebox and get us a quart of beer," Dave said. "Bring down four glasses."

"I'll help," I said.

Sven and I went up. There was only one quart of beer. We brought it down and four glasses, and Dave poured the beer, a half a glass for Sven, full ones for Dad and him and me.

"Jack's going to work at the boat club," Dad said.

"Dad, I don't know if it'll be permanent," I said.

"Sure it will," Dad said. "You'll be aces, they're lucky to get a kid as smart as you."

"Sure," Dave said. "Skoal."

We drank some beer. I took a pretty small swallow. I wasn't too big on the taste of beer yet.

"So you're going to work for the swells?" Dave said.

"I guess so," I said.

"Well they've got plenty of swells out there. Your pop and I used to play dances out there all the time."

"I didn't know that," I said.

"Sure," Dad said. "Back three or four years ago, in '33 and '34 they had a lot of parties out there. They were too hoity-toity for the country club. It was more exclusive for them to put on their own parties at the boat club."

"Those people," Dave said, "they never got hurt in the depression. They just never seemed to run out of money; they always had it."

"They had some pretty snappy dances out there," Dad said.

"Your pop and I were pretty big with the swells in those days," Dave said. "How 'bout that?"

"You should have seen the maroon tuxedo Dave had, Jack. Velvet lapels and a silver stripe down the trousers. He knocked 'em dead with that."

"Heck, Jack, that wasn't anything compared with the one your father had. It was midnight blue with sequins on the lapels and so many ruffles and flounces on the shirt he could hardly reach around them to hold the trombone. He was absolutely beautiful to behold." He began to laugh. "One night up at the Copley Plaza in Boston your pop had taken a wee drop too much. He lost a lit cigarette down in those damn flounces and the next thing we knew he'd jumped off the bandstand trailing smoke and began squirting himself all over the chest with a seltzer bottle. After that the boys in the band began calling him Smokey."

You would think that hearing about something dumb your father did would make you feel bad, but it didn't. It was nice sitting around there, with the smell of sawdust all around, listening to them tell stories. It made me feel like we were sort of pals, even Sven.

Dad laughed. "We had a lot of good times in those days. Dave, you remember that gig up in Bar Harbor, around '28 or '29, when the heat went off in the club and we could hardly play?"

"Yeah," Dave said. "That was some night, kids. We kept telling the manager to for God's sake get us a little heater or something up on the bandstand, and he kept saying it would warm up pretty soon. But it didn't, and finally after the third set your pop and I put on our overcoats and mittens and played the last two sets that way. He fired us that night."

Listening to these stories made me feel kind of

sorry I was going to be a baseball player instead of a musician. It sounded like a lot of fun, being a musician.

"It didn't matter if we got fired in those days," Dad said. "There was always plenty of work. You remember that crazy gangster out in Utica? He loved our band, Jack, he was crazy about it. But the place was full of mobsters and a couple of times a week somebody would start shooting holes in the ceiling or blowing glasses off the tables just for fun. So we decided to quit, and he just kept raising our salaries higher and higher; and finally we had to sneak out of town on a 6 A.M. train, just to escape." He lifted up his glass and emptied it, and then he glanced at Dave's glass. It was about empty, too. "I could stand another glass of beer, Dave."

"That's it," Dave said. "If I'd known you were coming I'd have got some more."

"Let's send Jack down to the corner for another quart." He reached into his pocket, took out a dollar, and handed it to me." "You know where the store is, don't you, Jack?"

I took the dollar. All of a sudden it wasn't much fun listening to the stories anymore. How come he didn't bring out the dollar at supper time when we were out of milk? Couldn't he have spared a dime for a quart of milk?

We walked home later on. I didn't know how to feel about it. I just couldn't believe that my own father would hold out on milk for the kids so he could have a couple of beers. How could he be a nice guy and joke around with you and then do something like that? It didn't make sense. The only thing I could figure is that he wasn't paying any

40

attention when we were talking about the milk, or that he'd forgotten he had the dollar, or something. I decided that I'd better remind him of Sally's new outfit, just in case.

"Did Sally tell you what kind of an outfit she's picked out?" I said as we walked down Main Street.

He touched my arm and frowned, and we stood under the streetlight. "Sal's got her heart set on that new dress, hasn't she?" he said.

"I guess so," I said. "She wants to look good."

"I hope I can do something about it," he said. "I've got a lot of bills coming up."

I was curious about that. "What kind of bills?"

"I don't want you worrying about that, Jack. I'll worry about it."

"Maybe you shouldn't have promised it to her," I said.

He shook his head. "No," he said, "she should have it if we can possibly afford it." He sighed. "Times are just so bad. I ought to be on the road. There isn't any work around here. I ought to be in Boston or Philly or New York right now. Maybe even L.A. There's a lot of movie work out there. A trumpet player Dave Johnson knows went out there and he's making a fortune."

He was starting to go off into one of his dreams again, and I tried to stop him. "But, Dad, you always hear stories like that."

"No, Dave says this guy has more work than he can handle with the Hollywood studios. They make hundreds of movies a year out there, and they all have to have background music. They don't use little three-piece bands, either, but big orchestras with three or four trombones. Besides all the nightclub work and regular dates and all. Hollywood, that's where the big money is. That's where I ought to be right now."

"But, Dad, what would we do if you went out there?"

"Oh I don't know," he said. "I haven't thought about it. Maybe we'd all move out there. How'd you like that? The sun shines all the time, and we could have a house on the beach, and Sally could finally get her riding lessons — that's great horse country out there — and swimming all year round, and maybe we'd get a boat, too. There's the whole Pacific Ocean to swim in. You ought to see those sunsets, Jack, you sit in your own front yard and watch the waves lap onto the beach and the sun go down into the ocean."

I gave up.

He put his hand on my shoulder and gave it a squeeze. "That's what we ought to do," he said. "Go to L.A. Just pick up and leave." He patted my arm. "Let's think about it."

On Saturday morning I got Sally to go over to Old Man Conklin's store and tell him that I was sick, I had some bug and was throwing up all night. She didn't like doing my dirty work for me, but she knew that if she was going to have a chance of marrying some rich man's son, I had to get the job out at the boat club, so she did it. I left at seven thirty, hitched a ride, and got out there before eight. The place was dead quiet, only the sound of the halyards slapping on the masts of the boats tied up at the docks as they rocked in the little waves. The only person around was Mr. Slater.

"We're supposed to open the bar from midday

until after the evening rush, but these bloody kids'll be coming in arsking for soda pop soon as they get out here, and I usually give it to 'em. You've got to keep an oiye on the bloody rarscals, they'll lift the stuff out of the cooler when you're not lookin', and 'arf the time they don't 'ave any money, so you'll 'ave to learn their names." Suddenly he realized that he was talking as if I was going to be there for a long time, and he said, "Well, you won't 'ave to worry about that today. First things first. I want you to sweep the place down and mop it — the club room, the porch, the observation deck, the lockers, and the whole bloody place. I'm going to be in my office with the insurance adjuster all morning and I don't want to be interrupted by some snooty kid 'oo wants a soda pop."

He showed me where the mops and brooms were, and I started swabbing the place down. I really worked hard at it, trying to do it fast but thoroughly, so he'd see what a good worker I was. For the first hour or so there weren't too many people around. It was nice and peaceful. When I went up onto the observation deck to clean it, I could see how beautiful it was — the lake sparkling in the sun, the breeze blowing the pine smell around, and back down the driveway, some people in white clothes flashing around the tennis courts.

At ten o'clock a bunch of kids came over for a tennis class, and after that I got pretty busy dishing out the soda pop and collecting the nickels. At eleven-thirty Mr. Slater came out of his office and began setting up the bar. He gave me a little white mess jacket and showed me how to set things up — cutting up strips of orange and lemon peel for fancy drinks, filling the ice wells, seeing that the glasses were cleaned, and so forth. Around noon people began coming in from sailing or tennis wanting drinks, and we were pretty busy until two o'clock when the last of them had gone home for lunch. I didn't mix any drinks; mostly I washed glasses and cleaned up the bar, kept the ice wells filled, and saw that there was enough cold beer and soda in the icebox. But whenever I could I watched to see how Mr. Slater made drinks. It didn't seem too hard, and I made up my mind that I would learn how, too. It was terrific experience; a good bartender could probably always get a job.

In the afternoon it was more of the same. I cleaned up the morning mess, and toward the end of the afternoon I walked around the docks and the porch picking up bottles and glasses and paper that people had left around. Mr. Slater said, "I'm particularly about keeping things tidy." At five o'clock when the boats began coming in, we had another rush at the bar, which lasted until around seven-thirty. Then we cleaned up, locked the liquor cabinet, and got ready to go home. Mr. Slater zinged open the cash register and counted out my pay, three dollars. Then he slapped me on the shoulder. "Busy day tomorrow," he said. "Races every Sunday, and they'll be out in force, especially if there's a wind. Be here at eight sharp." And that's how I learned I'd got the job.

Of course it ruined the weekends completely as far as having any fun, because by the time I'd finished putting in a twelve-hour day I was pretty exhausted and not much interested in anything but having my supper and going to bed. But I was making six dollars for the weekend, plus usually another couple of dollars in tips. We put the tips into a little jar on the back bar. Mr. Slater kept most of them, but he generally gave me two or three dollars out of the jar, depending on how much had come in. So I was making more than I had been at Conklin's, and my afternoons were free for baseball practice. Mostly free, anyway. Sometimes they had receptions or cocktail parties at the boat club during the week, but not too often. But to be honest, I didn't really mind giving up my weekends. It was pretty nice to be down there at the club, where everything was so bright and clean. The truth was, it was a lot nicer being rich than poor. It gave me a feeling of importance to be associated with the rich.

Mr. Slater was more cynical about the rich, though. He was always pointing out this man and that man who was loaded with dough — the owner of a big spinning mill or a famous lawyer or something — and he'd be proud about knowing them. But he'd be snotty about them, too. He'd say, "See that old dame over there? Got piles, knee-deep in the old simoleons, but she can 'ardly read nor write. 'Usband found 'er checking 'ats in a speakeasy during prohibition and she milked 'im dry and left 'im." Or he'd say, "See that old crock over there, the one with the straw 'at? Worth ten million, owns 'arf of Beacon 'Ill. Wets 'is bed."

Nobody but me and the groundskeepers called him Mr. Slater. Everybody in the club, including the kids, called him Slater. It seemed like he was sort of halfway between the rich and us riffraff. He ran the boat club in the summer. Winters he was assistant manager of a big golf club in Palm Beach,

Florida. "Ought to see the gentry we have down there," he said. "Mykes this lot look like pikers."

Meanwhile, baseball practice had started. I could see right away that I was going to have trouble. There were seven or eight good infielders in the high school, and they'd only keep five, besides the first baseman: the regular shortstop, third baseman, second baseman, and two infield subs. I wasn't too worried about my fielding — I was pretty good at that. The older guys had stronger arms than I did because they were bigger, but my arm was okay. It was my hitting that worried me. Hitting against some big seventeen-year-old guy wasn't nearly as easy as going up there against kids my own age. These guys could throw real curves, not the dinky little wrinkles I'd been seeing in junior high school. It was going to take getting used to.

The second weekend out at the club I found the wallet. I was out in the parking lot, which was between the back of the clubhouse and the grove of pine trees which screened off the tennis courts. I guess the rich didn't like the riffraff to see them play tennis. The older kids who belonged to the club used to sneak beer and drink it out there in the parking lot where their parents couldn't see them, and they always left their bottles around for me to pick up Sunday morning. I was going along picking up empties and putting them into a cardboard box when I spotted it — a new wallet, very thin and fancy.

I picked it up. There was a driver's license in a little isinglass window. I opened it up. Inside there were some membership cards for clubs. There was also a lot of money. I straightened up and looked casually around. There was nobody in sight. I glanced over at the clubhouse. Besides the back door there were four windows along the rear of the clubhouse — two for the locker rooms and two for the storeroom. In my quick glance I didn't see anybody looking out of them, but it's hard to tell from a distance whether there's anybody in a window or not. I walked casually over to where the cardboard box was sitting on the gravel, knelt down, and slipped the wallet in under some bottles. Then I picked up the box and carried it slowly off toward the far side of the parking lot where the grove of pine trees was, as if I were still looking for bottles. I went a little ways into the pine grove, set the box down, and looked around. There were a couple of people on the courts, but they were down at the other end, and even if they looked over, they wouldn't have been able to see what I was doing.

I took the wallet out of the box. My hands were shaking. I knew there was more money in that wallet than I'd ever seen before, but I didn't know how much. I spread it open and without taking the money out, flipped through the bills one at a time. There were two fifties, a twenty, three tens, and four singles — a hundred and fifty-four dollars altogether. I'd never even known that there were fifty dollar bills. I knew about hundreds, because I'd seen them in the movies, but fifties I'd never heard of, much less held one in my hand. Oh, it was a lot of money; it scared me, but it thrilled me, too. I could do a lot of things with that much money. I could buy Sally her dress, and me a new baseball glove; but mainly, it could keep the family from getting split up, for a while at least.

But taking the money would be stealing, and I

didn't know that I had the nerve to do it. Would I do it? It would be pretty easy to stick the money in my pocket and just drop the wallet at the edge of the pine grove where somebody else would find it. I wondered what they'd do then? I'd gotten my finger-prints all over it, but it didn't seem likely that they'd go the trouble of fingerprinting a lot of people to find out who'd taken the money — although you never could tell. If I was going to take the money, it would be better to get rid of the wallet altogether. That way whoever owned it wouldn't ever be sure where he'd lost it. I mean he might think that he'd dropped it by the docks and it fell into the water, or maybe he'd lost it somewhere else altogether. But how could I get rid of it? The best way would be to burn it in the incinerator we had in the parking lot for getting rid of papers and stuff. Or throw it way out into the lake with a stone tied onto it. Or dig a hole in the pines and bury it. The trouble with these ideas was that they meant carrying the wallet around with me for a while, or at least hiding it someplace until I could burn it or whatever I decided to do. That was pretty risky all right. Once they caught me with the wallet on me they'd accuse me of having stolen it. I might even get into trouble with the police. No, that wasn't a good idea, either.

I stood there thinking. I had to do something with the wallet in a couple of minutes. If I didn't get back into the clubhouse with my box of empty bottles soon, Mr. Slater would begin wondering where I was. I started to take the money out of the wallet. A little scared thrill went over me, and quickly I pushed the money back. I wanted it so; but it scared me. I pulled it back out, and this time I got it as far

48

as my hip pocket; but just feeling all that money in my own pocket scared me worse. Quickly I took it out of my pocket again. And then all at once an idea flashed over me. Carefully I put the money back in the wallet, and looked at the driver's license in the isinglass window. The name on it was Hobart Price Waterman. The name sounded sort of familiar, but I couldn't quite remember who he was. Probably somebody Mr. Slater had pointed out for some reason. I closed the wallet, stuck it into my back pocket, walked across the parking lot and through the back door to the clubhouse.

Mr. Slater was sitting in his office, going over his accounts. I knocked on the doorjamb. He looked up. I took the wallet out of my back pocket. "I found this in the parking lot, Mr. Slater," I said. "I think it belongs to Mr. Waterman." I threw that in just so Mr. Slater would realize I knew who it belonged to and wouldn't try to keep the wallet himself.

Mr. Slater stood up, took the wallet, and looked into it. "Phew," he said. He closed the wallet, put it in his own pocket, and then he gave me a quick funny look. "Did you count the money?"

If I said no, he might decide to take some himself. "Well, I didn't think I ought to do that," I said, "but it seemed like there must be way over a hundred dollars."

"Yes," he said. "I'd reckon it to be that." He looked at me and I looked at him. "Roight, Jack. Good boy. I'll ring Mr. Waterman and let him know we've got 'is wallet. Let's see if 'e gives you anythin' for your trouble."

I left and went back outside to pick up bottles around the docks. I was worried about what Mr.

Slater might do. Suppose he decided to take the money? Or suppose he decided to tell Mr. Waterman that he'd found the wallet himself. There wouldn't be much I could do about it if he did. I mean if I told Mr. Waterman that Mr. Slater was a liar, Mr. Slater would be sure to find out, and he'd fire me. So Mr. Slater could easily cheat me if he wanted to.

But he didn't. That afternoon a man came over to me when I was getting the bar set up for the evening rush. I'd served him drinks the weekend before. He was a pretty big drinker, in fact, although he was maybe around my dad's age, and athletic-looking. "You the boy who turned in my wallet?"

"Yes, sir," I said.

He gave me that same funny look Mr. Slater had given me. "A lot of people wouldn't have done that."

"I wasn't brought up that way," I said.

He nodded. Then he took the wallet out of his coat pocket, took out one of the tens, and handed it to me. "Get yourself a present on me," he said.

"Thank you, sir," I said. I'd never owned a ten-dollar bill before, and I folded it up carefully and put it into my back pocket. I knew exactly what I was going to do with it. I was going up to Boston, buy myself a new baseball glove, and then go over to Fenway Park to see the Red Sox play. It would be a terrific thing to do. But the most important thing wasn't the ten dollars. It was that people around the club would trust me, they would say what an honest kid I was. And that would make it a lot easier to get away with taking stuff, if I decided to.

I didn't get home until after nine that night. The wind had been down all day and the races had taken a lot longer than they usually did, even though they used the short course, so that there were still a lot of people in the club by eight o'clock. I was tired and I was hungry, and I went right into the kitchen to see what there was to eat. Dad was out someplace — I hoped on a gig, not at the Colonial — and Sally was out, too, probably over at Margene Sheckley's trying on lipstick. There was some bread and a dish of leftover baked beans in the icebox, so I made a sandwich of baked beans and mayonnaise, which is one of my favorites. There was milk, too; and I was sitting there gobbling up my dinner and feeling pretty tired when the baby came into the kitchen.

There were dirt streaks on his face, and his eyes were red, and I could tell he had been crying.

51

"What's the matter, Bab — Henry?" I said. He hated being called Baby and we were trying to stop.

"Sally says I have to go to Chicago to live with Uncle Edgar." He stood there looking at me with his arms folded across his chest, trying not to cry.

"Are you sure Sally told you that?"

"Yes."

I was surprised. I didn't think Sally would have done that, unless maybe she was mad. "Are you sure?"

"She said it to Margene."

"Oh," I said. "Well, that's what you get for listening in."

"I wasn't listening in." He rubbed his eyes. "They were talking too loud in her room."

That explains it. "Well, they were just talking, Henry. Probably it won't happen."

"Would you come, too?"

"Henry, stop worrying about it. It isn't going to happen."

"You're lying," he said. He went on rubbing his eyes. He was half sore and half ready to cry, and I figured I better make it sound like I was telling the truth.

"Well the thing is, Henry, what Sally meant is that it *could* happen. I mean if we really went broke, we might all have to go to live in different places. You might live with Uncle Edgar and Aunt Mabel, and maybe Sally would live with Grandpa down in New Orleans, and I might move in with somebody else. But that would be only if we really got broke."

"I won't go," he said. He let out a sudden sob and then he sucked it back in and sort of shuddered. A tear winked in his eye, but he refused to cry. "I'll run back home."

"Henry, stop worrying; it isn't going to happen." I hated saying that, because if it did, he'd blame me; but I had to cheer him up.

"Well, Sally said."

"Sally doesn't know what she's talking about." I wished she'd keep her mouth shut when the baby was around.

"Well she said."

"Well I'm saying, and I'm bigger than her. Now stop worrying about it."

That seemed to convince him; he cheered up a little and sat down at the table with me. "Gimme a bite of your sandwich."

I was pretty hungry and I didn't want to give him any, but considering that he was feeling bad, I had to. I held out the sandwich and he took a bite. "Eeyah, pew," he said. He spit the bite out onto the table. "What kind of a sandwich is that?"

"Damn it, don't waste my sandwich."

"Eeyah," he said. "That's a puky sandwich."

"Why didn't you ask what it was before you started to hog it up? Now clean it up, I'm trying to eat dinner."

He picked up the half-chewed bite and threw it in the garbage pail. "It's a baked bean sandwich. Whoever heard of a baked bean sandwich?"

"I did," I said. I got the rest of the beans out of the icebox and made another sandwich. "Now go away and stop bothering me."

"Please, I won't bother you anymore."

"Don't you have any homework?"

"We never have any homework in the third grade," he said. "Listen, Jack, Sally says Dad's going to buy her a new outfit. Maybe he'll buy me something."

"Henry, you've got to quit listening in all the time."

"I can't help it if they talk too loud."

"Well shut your ears next time."

"I can't shut my ears. How can you shut your ears?"

I was pretty tired of talking with him. "I don't know, now stop bothering me."

"Listen, Jack, if Dad buys Sally a dress, will he buy me something?"

"He might not buy Sally a dress. He just said he *might* buy her one."

"Sally said he promised."

I was beginning to lose my temper. "Well we don't have any money. We're almost broke." Suddenly I realized I shouldn't have said that, because it might give him the idea all over again that he'd have to go to Chicago. But he'd cheered up and forgotten about that, so I told him to go to bed, it was past his bedtime, and he went. Sally wasn't home yet, although she should have been, because it was getting towards her bedtime, too. But she knew that Dad was out and she could get away with it. So I brought the record player into the kitchen, where it wouldn't disturb the baby, and set it up on the kitchen table. Then I went back to the living room to get some records. They were kept in a big fancy cherry wood cabinet that Dad had custom made once. It cost fifty dollars to have it made. Mom had really hit the roof when she had found out how much it cost — you could buy plain record cabinets for twelve dollars, she had said. But Dad had said his usual thing, that it was a business expense. I have to admit, I loved looking at all those records lined up there in that cabinet. There were over five hundred of them, all divided into categories — classical, jazz, cowboy, marches, popular, foreign, and so forth. Dad had them all arranged alphabetically so you could easily find any record you wanted. His records was the one thing Dad was organized about. That record cabinet was the nicest thing in the living room. The rest of the furniture was old wornout stuff left over from before the depression. The sofa had a couple of busted springs so it made a big sag hole for your fanny at one end. The morris chair had a fanny sag, too, and the coffee table was full of cigarette burns from when Dad had some of his musician friends over to drink beer and listen to records. So it was nice to have at least one decent thing in the living room, even if he shouldn't have spent all that money on it.

I crouched down in front of the cabinet and thought about what I wanted to hear. When I was a little kid I used to like to listen to the Sousa marches. Dad had a lot of them, because of the good trombone parts. But now either I liked to listen to Debussy or swing. Tonight I didn't feel much like Debussy. So I looked through the swing records, sliding them partway out so I could see the labels and then keeping out the ones I decided to listen to. I got Goodman's "Bugle Call Rag," Bob Crosby's "Gin Mill Blues," Shep Fields's "This Year's Kisses."

Then I took the records back to the kitchen, put on "Gin Mill Blues," and sat there listening and leaning back in my chair with my feet up on the kitchen table, which I wasn't supposed to do. When I listened to records I liked to really get deep into them, close my eyes and shut off the world and float around in the music. I imagined it would be like getting into a diving suit and drifting around underwater looking at all the colorful fish swimming around through the beautiful coral and junk. You really had to concentrate to get down into the music, though. If a car honked or somebody started bustling around, you came up out of it. That's why I liked to get really leaned back when I listened. The best thing was to lie down, which is what I did when I was listening in the living room. But I didn't feel like lying on the kitchen floor. To be frank, it was pretty dirty. We were supposed to take turns sweeping it, but we always got into arguments about whose turn it was and half the time it didn't get done.

So I sat there leaning back, but I couldn't get concentrated. There were too many things going around in my head, sort of chasing themselves one after another. There were things like Dad keeping that dollar for beer when we didn't have any milk. I hadn't gotten over that, it still bothered me. I guess in a way I understood, he probably got pretty tired of spending every bit of money he got on rent and milk and potatoes and sweaters for us kids. But he was the father, wasn't he? He didn't have to have any children if he didn't want to, did he? Of course maybe having us was Mom's idea and she talked him into it, which she normally could do. Or used to be able to do, anyway. Still, he was supposed to be the father.

Another thing chasing through my head was the poor baby crying about maybe being sent off to Chicago to live with Uncle Edgar and Aunt Mabel. I wouldn't want to live with them, I can tell you that. They were very strict and religious. If Henry had to live there, he'd have to dress up all the time, and cut his meat right, and keep his room neat as a pin, and hang up his clothes in the closet every night when he went to bed, which is pretty silly if you're just going to put them back on again in the morning. I mean if the lights are out and you're probably asleep anyway, who cares if your clothes are flopped over a chair?

So that was another thing chasing through my head. And then there was one more — the whole business of finding that guy's wallet and thinking about stealing. It scared me even to think about it, that's the truth. And the point was, would I actually steal something if I had the chance? I don't mean swiping gum from Pete's Smoke Shop, but something big. Suppose Mr. Waterman decided that I was a terrifically honest kid and hired me to work around his place every afternoon — you know, left me there cutting the grass or scrubbing the kitchen floor or something. In a rich man's house there were bound to be a lot of things you could steal that they wouldn't notice. Well. I wasn't sure, I'd never been in a rich man's house, but I'd seen them in movies. Of course you couldn't trust the movies, exactly. I knew they made a lot of that junk up. But it just seemed like it must be so, there must be a lot of stuff around a rich man's house that you could easily steal.

Actually, you could do plenty of stealing around the boat club, if you wanted to. There was a lot of expensive stuff lying around. I could easily steal an outboard motor some night — just climb over the iron gate, get the motor, climb back up to the top of the iron gate, hoist the motor up on a rope, and then lower it down the other side. If I had somebody with a car to help me, I probably could steal a whole bunch of motors. Or you could come over at night in a rowboat and take some away. Why, in fact, it wouldn't be any trouble to steal a whole boat. Some of those boats were worth hundreds of dollars.

Then another thing was, there was all that money in the cash register. Mr. Slater counted it up every night, and the amount had to match with the tape. But you could always forget to ring up a sale, or ring up the wrong amount by mistake. Sometimes when we got real busy Mr. Slater would leave the cash drawer open, lay the bills on the little shelf in front of the register, and make change without ringing it up. He'd ring it all up later, but in the meantime there was a chance that you would make a mistake, or a five would drop to the floor or something. I mean if you were working the bar by yourself with nobody watching it seemed to me that you could easily steal a few dollars every night without getting caught. But the point was, would I do it? When it came down to it, and I saw some jewels or something in a rich man's house, would I have the guts to shove them into my pocket? Would I have the guts to cheat on the cash register in the boat club? I didn't know.

I sat there trying to listen to "Gin Mill Blues" with all these ideas chasing around in my head. I wished they would go away. I was too tired to think about them. I just wanted to concentrate on listening to records. I wondered if Dad would be coming home soon, or if he was on a gig and wouldn't get home until one or two. If the gig ran until midnight, he usually would go out and have a beer with the guys in the band. If it ran later, most of the guys would usually want to go right home. I wondered, were all these ideas running around in his head, too? I figured he didn't think about these things too much. The way he was, he only seemed to think about what he wanted to think about. To tell the truth, it seemed like I was more of the father than he was. I mean it was me who was doing all the worrying, and cheering up the baby, and trying to keep Sal from getting her hopes up about the new outfit, and wondering about stealing money so that the family wouldn't have to break up. Thinking that I was more of the father than Dad was gave me a pretty funny feeling. How could you be the father of your own father? It wasn't very natural. But still, it seemed like it was true.

With all of these thoughts rolling around in my head I finally gave up on trying to listen to records. I made up my bed on the daybed, left a note on the kitchen table for Sally telling her not to wake me up when she came in, and went to bed.

But I didn't go to sleep right away, and so I decided to have a daydream to keep me from being bored until I dozed off. For a minute I lay there trying to decide what kind of daydream to have. I thought about having a stealing daydream; but I was kind of bored with them. Then I thought about having a millionaire daydream, where it turned out that some rich man was really my father, but I wasn't too interested in that, either. So I decided to have a baseball daydream:

"What a situation," the announcer shouts. "Bases loaded with two down in the last of the ninth, the Red Sox behind five to two, and no pinch hitters left except this young kid Lundquist they've just brought up from the minors, and the whole season rides on this game. Just think of the pressure on that kid. We don't know much about him, folks, except that he was hitting .367 in the minors and the Sox brought him up a couple of weeks ago just to give him a little experience. And what an experience. The crowd is on their feet, roaring. Ruffing stands in. He stares down at Lundquist. Lundquist wriggles the bat a little. He looks a little like Bobby Doerr the way he stands in there. Ruffing is into his motion. He pitches. Lundquist takes called strike one. Lundquist isn't particularly big — five foot ten, weighs a hundred and sixty-five. Now Ruffing's ready. He throws. Lundquist takes a ball low and outside. The crowd is a little quieter, expectant. Ruffing has a look over at third. He bluffs a throw. Now he's on the rubber. He's into his windup. It's a swing and a miss. Lundquist took a healthy cut and got fooled on a breaking ball that tailed away from him. Two and one. Ruffing rubs up the ball. The crowd is hushed. One more strike and it's all over until next year for the Red Sox. Ruffing sets and pitches. Lundquist takes a fast ball high and inside. Ruffing tried to come back at him, but the kid wouldn't bite. Two and two. Ruffing turns around to check his outfield. He goes to the rubber, glances over at third, but makes no motion. Now he goes to the plate. Lundquist takes a fast ball that just missed the outside corner.

*Three and two. The crowd is dead quiet. I swear
you could hear a pin drop out here at Fenway.
It's about as dramatic a situation as you can have
in sports. Lundquist steps out, wipes some dirt
on his hands, and kicks the dirt out of his cleats.
I don't blame him for being a little nervous out
there — a nineteen-year-old kid in a situation like
this. Now he's back in. Ruffing sets. One more
strike and the Yankees wrap up another pennant.
Ruffing looks over to third. He winds and pitches.
There's a swing and a long drive out into left
field, it's going way back, I don't believe it. Selkirk
is racing toward the wall, and it's up and out of
here, a home run over the left-field wall and the
ball game is over. Foxx is in, Ferrell is in, Dahl-
gren is in, and Lundquist is jogging around third
heading for home. The crowd is in a pandemon-
ium, I've never seen anything like it, and Lundquist, this kid from the bushes, jumps on home
plate and the Red Sox win their first pennant since
1918."*

After a while I went to sleep.

I would have liked to have talked to somebody
about all my thoughts, but I didn't like the idea of
talking about Dad being kind of neglectful. I didn't
even like thinking about it.

I didn't even want to tell my best friend. My best
friend was Charlie Franks. He was a lefty and he
played first base on the junior high team. He was
going out for the high school team, too, but he was
having even more trouble than me hitting curve
balls. A lefty doesn't have so much trouble hitting a
righty's curves, so he was all right against righties,

but he'd never hit against a lefty who could throw a curve, and it was giving him a lot of trouble. He was pretty discouraged.

That Monday, the day after I got the ten-dollar bill from Mr. Waterman, we walked home from practice together. "Listen," I said, "I've got ten bucks. I found some guy's wallet out at the boat club, and he gave me ten bucks reward for turning it in."

"How much was in the wallet?"

"Over a hundred and fifty bucks." I tried to make it sound casual. "There were two fifties in it."

"Holy smoke," he said. "A hundred and fifty bucks. Why didn't you keep it?"

"I was afraid I might get caught. There might have been somebody looking out the window."

"God, a hundred and fifty bucks. I'd have taken it. Couldn't you have slipped the money into your pocket and then told them it was empty when you found it? They would have thought somebody had picked the guy's pocket and taken the money and thrown the wallet away."

I wished I'd thought of that, although I still don't think I'd have taken the chance. "I figured they wouldn't believe me," I said. Then I looked at him sort of sideways as we walked along. "Would you ever steal anything, Charlie? I don't mean swiping candy out of Pete's, I mean something big?"

"Sure, if I didn't think I'd get caught."

I didn't know if he was just boasting or would really do it. "Really? You wouldn't be scared to?"

"Well, I might be scared a little, but I'd do it. Especially if it belonged to some rich guy. A guy who carries around a hundred and fifty dollars in his wallet, to him it's like fifty cents. If you lost fifty cents, you'd be sorry about it, but it wouldn't kill you. The same with this guy. If he lost his hundred and fifty bucks, he'd be sorry about it, but he'd just go home and get some more out of his safe."

"Probably he'd keep his money in a bank."

"Those rich guys always have a safe full of money in their houses. Just in case of emergencies. Usually the safe is behind a picture."

I knew he got that from the movies. I figured a guy like Mr. Waterman would keep his money in a bank. "Well anyway," I said, "I figured I'd buy a glove. I figured I could get a good Higgins for six bucks." Suddenly something came to me, which was that I shouldn't buy a baseball glove at all; what I ought to do with my ten dollars was to buy Sally her outfit. But then I thought: why should I? I didn't promise her the dress, Dad did. I wouldn't have made such a promise. Why should I have to live up to his promises? Anyway, maybe he would get the outfit for her. Maybe he had some money saved for it. But I knew he didn't.

"Where are you going to buy the glove?" Charlie said.

"I didn't say I was going to buy it. I said I was *thinking* about it."

"That's what I'd do," Charlie said. "Buy a glove. If you don't spend it on something big like a glove, you'll just fritter it away on frappes and comic books."

"Maybe I ought to save it," I said.

"If you leave it lying around the house, you might lose it."

"Charlie, everybody doesn't lose as much stuff as you do." Being a lefty, Charlie is sort of nutty.

63

"I don't lose that much stuff."

"You lost your glove twice last year; you're always losing your sweater." He lost his sweater so much that sometimes his mother won't buy him another one for a while and makes him go to school without one to teach him a lesson.

"Well you can lose stuff, too. You might lose your ten bucks if you leave it around. I think you ought to buy the glove."

I sure wanted that glove. "Well listen, Charlie," I said. "If I decide to do it, I'm going to get it in Boston. Do you want to go up with me? We could go to the Red Sox game."

"Sure," he said. "If I've got the money."

"It won't cost too much if you don't stuff yourself with hot dogs. Just the fifty-five cents to get in. We can hitchhike up and take the trolley out to Fenway."

"Sure," he said. "Let's check the schedule."

"The thing is," I said, "we'll have to go during the week. I have to work at the boat club on the weekends."

"We'll play hooky. We'll ditch school and hitchhike down."

So we went over to Charlie's house and looked up the schedule. The Red Sox were on a road trip, but they were coming home after the weekend. "Look, the Yankees are going to be in Boston next week," Charlie said. The Yankees were Boston's worst enemy. They hardly ever lost the pennant. "We can see Gehrig and DiMaggio. Have you ever seen Gehrig?"

"No," I said. "I've never seen the Yankees."

"We ought to go to one of those games. Maybe Wednesday."

"If I decide. I haven't decided yet, Charlie."

I thought about it all week. Charlie kept after me to make up my mind. He was eager to go. I sure wanted to. It was a pretty big deal to go up to Boston for the ball game. I'd only been to Fenway Park three times, and once to see the Bees. I mean you ended up spending at least two dollars, between trolley fares and the admission and stuff to eat, and then of course you had bus fare, unless you hitched. Oh, I wanted to go all right.

But how could I throw away money on a baseball glove when we were out of milk half the time and Sally needed a new outfit? I kept trying to think of reasons each way. I mean on one side of it, I didn't make that promise to Sally, Dad did; and besides, a new baseball glove would help me get on the team and make all-state, so it was a kind of investment for the family. If I made all-state, I would have a chance to get signed up by a team and at least get into the minors, and then I'd be making money and could send some home. But the minute I thought of that, I realized it was like saying that the baseball glove was a business expense. I was pretty mixed up about it. Why was it up to me to take care of the family?

I still hadn't made up my mind by the weekend when I went down to the boat club. It had been a month since I'd started working there, and I'd gotten used to it. Sweeping and mopping was pretty boring, but it only took me a couple of hours each morning to get that part of the job done. Then I'd set up the bar and bring out beer or liquor if we needed it. That was more interesting — it was more of a grown-up thing to do, and I'd pretend I was a real bartender and was going to run the bar on my own. In the afternoon, after the noon bar business was over, I'd eat my lunch, which was usually a couple of bologna and cheese sandwiches I made at home before I left in the morning. There were always potato chips and pretzels and junk like that around, and Mr. Slater didn't mind if I drank a Moxie out of the cooler, which was my favorite kind of soda pop. In the afternoon I'd wash up the lunchtime glasses and pick up the bottles and trash around the docks and the clubhouse, and then there wouldn't be too much to do until the evening bar rush, unless there was a liquor delivery. I would stand on the porch by the clubhouse door, where I could keep an eye on the bar and watch the races if it was Sunday, or just linger there and look at the sailboats and listen to the rich people talk. It just amazed me how much money they had. You'd hear a couple of young guys, maybe seventeen or eighteen, talking about whether they ought to buy a DeSoto or a Pontiac, just the way I'd talk about what kind of baseball glove to buy. Or they'd be talking about some trip they were going on, like taking the Twentieth Century Limited out to the Coast, or even about some airplane trip, as if it was nothing at all. Even the little kids talked the same way. Once I heard one kid say to his friend, "We just got back from Europe, did you go yet?" And the other one said, "We didn't go yet, we're going to Paris in June." And the first one said, "Yeah, we went to Paris, it was boring as usual."

This particular Saturday the weather was cloudy and chilly. There was a good wind, so a lot of boats were out, but there weren't very many people hanging around the club. When they came in they usually went right home, instead of coming in for a drink or something. During the slow period in the afternoon I spent a lot of time standing by the door onto the porch, watching the boats. It seemed like a great thing to be able to skip over the lake like that, slicing along through the waves. I wished I could be out there too. I figured that if I got the job full time in the summer maybe I could get somebody to teach me. Maybe if I learned how to sail I could help give the sailing lessons to the little kids. Maybe I could learn tennis and give kids lessons in that, too. Giving lessons would be a lot better than sweeping up and picking up bottles. Oh, there were lots of possibilities for jobs in the boat club. I mean maybe I could even become steward some day. If I didn't get into the majors.

The day went along. We set up the bar for the evening business, but there was hardly any, and at seven o'clock, Mr. Slater said, "No point in us 'angin' around any longer, Jack. Do your clean up and push off." He went into his office and I washed the glasses and put them away, took out the trash and burnt it in the incinerator in the parking lot, and swabbed off the bar. I hung up my mess jacket, put on my sweater, said good-bye to Mr. Slater, and started down the driveway. As I got down near the gate, a car came up the driveway going toward the clubhouse. I wondered if it was somebody who wanted a drink, and that reminded me that I hadn't put any soda pop in the cooler. Sometimes people would come out for an early sail and would want to take some pop or beer out in their boats with them. You had to put some in the cooler the night before to make sure it would be cold for them. So I turned around and went back up the driveway. There was a

1935 Ford standing in the parking lot next to Mr. Slater's station wagon. I went through the back door of the clubhouse and into the storeroom. There was a big stack of soda cases in the middle of the room waiting for me to put them away. I would have to take some out of each case so there'd be an assortment on ice — some Moxie, some Hires root beer, some coke, some ginger ale. I started to reach down the top case, when suddenly I heard voices. Mr. Slater was in the main room talking to someone. I could hear the voices pretty well, so I knew that they were standing at the bar, which backed up against the storeroom.

"Ta, Eddie," Mr. Slater said. "You're a gentleman and a scholar."

"Don't spend it all in one place," the other voice said.

"Not very bloody likely," Mr. Slater said. "Cheerio."

They clinked glasses. I knew who Eddie was. He wasn't a member of the club, but one of the liquor wholesalers. Why was he giving Mr. Slater money? It ought to be the other way around. I started to pull the case down.

"You know, Eddie, I loik you," Mr. Slater said. "I wish we could do more business together."

Eddie said something, but I couldn't hear what. I stood there quietly, trying to listen.

Mr. Slater said, "Perhaps we can. . . ." I couldn't hear the rest.

I was pretty curious. I knew I'd be in a lot of trouble if I got caught listening in, but I was curious. I slipped over to the storeroom door and sort of put my head out into the little hall there.

"Umph," Eddie said. There was a little silence and then he said, "Times are hard. It's rough getting up the twenty a month as it is."

"Oh, come on now, Eddie, twenty dollars isn't very much. Guzman is contributing thirty-five to the cause."

"Guzman does twice as much business as I do."

"That's exactly what I mean, Eddie," Mr. Slater said. "Guzman knows how to build his business."

I knew what it was all about. It was kickbacks, bribes, whatever you wanted to call it. Mr. Slater was making Eddie pay him twenty dollars a month to be allowed to sell liquor to the boat club. Dad used to tell us about kickbacks. Sometimes the guy who hired bands at a nightclub or a dance hall would make the leader pay him so much money if he wanted to be hired. It wasn't just in the music business, Dad said. It happened in all kinds of businesses, and I guess with the depression you weren't too surprised if people cheated. I didn't know for sure, but probably the way it worked was, Mr. Slater took a twenty dollar kickback from Eddie, and then he wouldn't make a fuss about it when Eddie put something extra on the liquor bill. In the end, Mr. Slater wasn't paying the liquor bill, the club members were.

"Well," Eddie said, "maybe I could manage another five."

"Oh come on, Eddie, you can do better than that. Make it ten. You 'ave to give something to get something in this world."

"It's pretty hard," Eddie said.

I knew I'd better not get caught now. If Mr. Slater realized that I knew he was taking kickbacks, he'd fire me right off the bat. He'd tell the members he caught me stealing or something, so in case I told them about the kickbacks they wouldn't believe me, and that would be the end of that.

"I'll tell you what," Eddie said. "Let's make it another five and see how it goes before we go up to ten."

"Agreed," Mr. Slater said. "Let's have another drink on that."

"A quick one."

I pulled back inside the storeroom and looked around. The stack of soda pop cases in the middle of the room was high enough for me to hide behind. I tiptoed back across the storeroom and ducked down behind the stack of cases. I heard Eddie's muffled voice say something like, "Down the hatch," and then footsteps began to come toward me. I pressed up against the cases. The two of them walked by the storeroom door and out into the parking lot. I could vaguely hear their voices and then the sound of a car motor start, and then Mr. Slater came back into the building and walked past the storeroom. I listened for his footsteps, and in a moment I realized that he was going into his office. I knew I ought to make a run for it — just slip out the back door and run down toward the gate. But I was curious. My heart was beating pretty hard. I tiptoed toward the storeroom door and stood there for a couple of seconds. There was a sound coming from Mr. Slater's office like a chair being moved. I slipped out into the hall and then down to the end, where I could look across the empty club room and into the office through the open door. I couldn't see much. Mr. Slater was standing on a chair, but all I could see was the lower part of his body. In a minute he jumped down. He was holding in his arms a sleeping bag, which I realized must have been up on one of the high shelves that lined the office. He dumped the bag down on the floor and unrolled it. Was he going to go to sleep in it? He didn't spread it out, though. When he got it partly unrolled he reached his hand down inside of it and pulled out a big brown paper envelope. Then he reached into his pocket, took out some money — at the distance I couldn't see how much — put it into the envelope, and slid the envelope back down into the sleeping bag. I knew what it was — it was his hiding place for his kickback money. I wondered how much was in it.

He rolled the sleeping bag up and climbed back up on the chair. I turned and began to tiptoe back down the hall. I figured I could slip outside and then make a dash for it across the parking lot and down the driveway to safety. I got halfway down the corridor and suddenly I heard Mr. Slater's footsteps coming across the club room. I didn't have time to make a dash for it anymore; he was bound to spot me going across the parking lot. My heart beating fast, I slipped into the storeroom, tiptoed across, and ducked around behind the stack of cases. And at that moment Mr. Slater reached the storeroom door and stopped. "Bloody kid," he said. "Left the light on agine." The light switch was by the door. Mr. Slater snapped it and suddenly I was standing in the dark. Then the door swung closed and clicked shut. I waited, keeping my breath low. There was a sort of rattling and then a scratching, and I knew that Mr. Slater was putting his key into the storeroom door lock. In a moment there was a little click and I was locked in.

I went on standing there behind the soda cases,

but allowing myself to breathe a little more noisily. I heard him go out the back door and shut it; and finally I heard the sound of the car starting up. I listened to the tires crunch down the gravel driveway, and then he was gone and there was no sound at all except the faint swash-swash of the waves on the beach and the slapping of halyards on masts.

Now what? I could spend the night in the storeroom, of course. They wouldn't get worried about me at home. If I wasn't home at her bedtime, Sally would think that I was over at Charlie Franks'. Dad had the Elks Club gig and he'd sleep in the living room as usual when he came in late, and not realize that I wasn't home. Anyway, he didn't notice very much where we were. Usually it was one of us kids that reminded him that somebody wasn't around. I mean if I wasn't home for supper, he wouldn't pay much attention to it, but Sally would know where I was supposed to be and remind him of it.

So that wasn't the problem. I'd just call up in the morning and let them know I was okay. The real problem was having Mr. Slater open up the storeroom in the morning and find me there. Then I'd really be in trouble. He'd want to know how come I didn't shout or something when he switched the lights off; and in the end he'd conclude that I'd been spying on him and Eddie, or planning to steal stuff, or who knows what. He'd fire me on the spot and maybe get the police into it, too.

I had to get out. There was some dim light coming through the storeroom windows, but being overcast the way it was, there was no moon or stars. I felt my way around the stack of soda cases and worked my way carefully over to the door. When I reached it, I grabbed the knob and gave it a twist. It turned, but when I pulled on the door it didn't budge. I kept the knob turned and gave it a hard jerk. It didn't give any at all.

So that was no good. If I'd had a wrecking bar or even a hammer, I might have been able to pry the door open. The boat club owned a lot of tools for people to use in making repairs on their boats, but Mr. Slater kept them locked up in his office. People would walk off with them otherwise.

I stood away from the door and looked around. There was nothing to see but the darkness, and two rectangular gray patches where the windows were. They were set about six feet up the wall. In a storeroom you don't want a lot of windows getting in the way of the shelves. Besides, big windows make it easy for people to break in. These windows were pretty small, but they were big enough for me to squeeze through.

Being alone there in the dark was making me feel trapped. I was beginning to think about things like rats rustling around in the dark or bugs and huge spiders crawling on the floor. I just wanted to get out of there. I felt my way back to the soda cases, pulled three of them down, and stacked them under one of the windows. I climbed up on the cases and began feeling around the frame. It was one of those windows that was hinged on the bottom and tilted inward when you opened it. I guess it was mostly meant for air. I felt along the top until I found the catch. I pulled it. It slid back easily enough. Then I tugged on it to pull the window open. It didn't budge. I figured it was stuck, because those windows hadn't been opened for a while. I gave the catch handle a good hard tug. Still nothing happened. I tugged hard. Nothing. I let go of the catch and began feeling around the edges of the frame, and in a moment I knew what the problem was: the window had been nailed shut. I figured that Mr. Slater had nailed it up after the robbery. I shivered. I was pretty sure that he'd have nailed up the other one, too, but I decided to try anyway. I got off the boxes, slid them over to the other window, climbed up again and felt around. That one was nailed shut, too.

I felt pretty sunk. There was only one thing left to do — break one of the windows. I sure didn't want to do that, though. It would stir up an awful uproar in the morning. Mr. Slater would figure there had been another robbery — but that gave me an idea. Quickly I stepped down from the cases. Then I pulled down the stack, scattering the cases around the floor. I ripped open a couple of the cases and scattered some bottles around. I knew that in the end I'd have to pick up the mess in the morning, but that didn't worry me, as long as nobody thought I'd made it in the first place. Then I fumbled around on the floor until I found a soda bottle, wrapped my sweater around it, and banged it at the window. There was a crash. I stood there waiting for a minute to see if anybody had heard the noise; but there were no sounds. Quickly I unwrapped my sweater from the bottle, and holding the bottle by the neck, chipped the jagged pieces of glass from around the edge of the window. Then I laid my sweater over the bottom edge of the frame, just in case there was still some glass there, hoisted myself upwards, and sort of slid out the window head forward and tumbled onto the gravel of the parking lot. I grabbed my sweater out of the window and began to run, not down the driveway in case somebody might come up it, but through the pines and along the edge of the tennis courts. When I got to the big iron gate, I stopped and waited. There were no cars coming along the road. Quickly I shinnied up the gate and swung over the top. Then I slid down the other side and began to jog along the road toward home. And it was about that time that I noticed my hand was wet and slippery, and I realized that I'd given myself a pretty good cut across the palm somewhere along the line. And what was Mr. Slater going to think when he found the window to his storeroom broken and me coming in to work with a cut hand?

5

I wrapped my handkerchief around my hand to stop the bleeding as much as I could and trotted along quickly until I got to the edge of town where the streetlights began. When I got under the first light I stopped, unwrapped my handkerchief, and had a look. It was pretty well messed up. There was blood all over my hand and some on the other hand and blood on my sweater from where I'd been holding it. There were smears of blood on my shirt where I'd touched it and some drops of blood on my pants. It wasn't a very deep cut, but it had bled a lot because I hadn't noticed it. By now the bleeding was mostly stopped, though. So I wrapped the handkerchief around my hand again and went on home.

I was surprised to see Dad sitting there in the living room. "I thought you had the Elks Club tonight."

"It got canceled." Then he saw my hand. "What happened to you?"

"I cut myself when I was washing the glasses. One of them broke in the bottom of the sink and I didn't see it."

"You'd better clean it up. Why didn't you put a bandage on it?"

"I did, but it came off on the way home and started bleeding again." Suddenly it occurred to me that there'd be blood all over the iron gate where I'd climbed it, and drops along the tennis court and maybe some around the broken window.

"Well make sure you put plenty of iodine on it."

I went into the bathroom, washed myself as best I could, and searched through the medicine cabinet for some Mercurochrome, which didn't sting as much as iodine. But there wasn't any, so I put on the iodine, which stung, and bandaged up the cut. Then I went back into the living room. "What's for supper?"

"Frank and beans. It's on the stove."

"Where's Sally?"

"I think she must be over at the Sheckleys'. She took the baby with her."

"We're supposed to call him Henry," I said.

"Henry," he said.

I went out into the kitchen. On the stove there was a pan with some cold beans in it. There were franks cut up into the beans. I was getting pretty tired of beans, but I was hungry. I lit the stove. It didn't seem to me that we were getting enough vitamins around there. We were always eating stuff like hash and canned stew and franks and beans. But I knew if I said anything to Sally about cooking more vegetables, she'd get sore and tell me that if I didn't like

77

the meals I could cook myself. Actually, Sally didn't cook all the time. Dad did sometimes when he was around, and I would take a turn sometimes. It was all kind of a problem because none of us knew how to cook. Naturally Mom had always done all the cooking. She'd taught Sally to cook a little, but mostly junk like angel food cake and fudge and brownies. We weren't eating stuff like that anymore.

The franks and beans began to bubble. I stirred it around until it was nice and steamy. Then I got out some milk, some bread and butter, and some ketchup. I dumped the franks and beans onto a plate, poured a huge slosh of ketchup over them, and sat down to eat. I'd got about halfway through when Dad came in and sat down at the kitchen table.

"Listen, Jack," he said, "who told the baby that he was going to Chicago to live with Uncle Edgar and Aunt Mabel?"

I got red. "I didn't tell him that," I said.

"Did Sally?"

I didn't want to blame Sally, but it was her dumbness for not being able to keep her mouth shut that caused it. "It wasn't Sally's fault. Henry was listening in when she was talking to Margene."

"What gave Sally the idea that Henry was going to have to go somewhere else to live?"

Anything I said would be wrong. "Don't blame me," I said. "I told Henry not to worry about it. I told him it wasn't going to happen."

"Jack, I want to know where this idea got started."

"Sally and I were just sort of talking."

"Talking? About what?"

"Well, I mean about going broke. What would happen if we went broke."

"And you decided that Henry would have to go live with Uncle Edgar? What else did you decide?"

I knew he was getting mad. I looked down at my plate and shoveled in some beans. "Oh, nothing. We were just talking."

"What else, Jack?"

I said in a low voice, "Well, we figured somebody would have to go to live down in New Orleans with Grandpa."

"And what gave you the idea that I couldn't take care of this family?"

"Don't get mad at *me*, Dad. I didn't do anything."

He shook his head. "You're always borrowing trouble, Jack. You're such a worrywart. Have we ever missed a meal around here? Have we ever had to sleep in the street? Now I don't want you getting the baby all upset with this stuff anymore. Right, Jack?"

"Why are you blaming me? It wasn't me."

"I know," he said. "But you started it. Stop being such a worrywart. Things generally work out in the end."

I just wanted to end the conversation and finish my supper. "All right, I won't anymore."

"And when Sally comes home, tell her, too."

"Why do I have to — "

"You started it," he said.

Then he went out of the room.

I buttered a piece of bread and went on eating. Having him get mad at me should have spoiled my dinner, but I was hungry, and it didn't. I went on eating, and pretty soon Sally and the baby came home. "Where have you been?" I said.

"Over at Margene's. What happened to your hand?"

"I cut it," I said.

"How?" Henry said. "Did it hurt?"

"I cut it on a broken glass," I said. "It's all right now."

"Hey, Jack," Henry said, "Dad told me I don't have to go to Chicago to live."

"Well I told you not to worry about it, Henry," I said.

"It's your bedtime, Henry," Sally said.

"I don't want to go to bed," he said.

"Damn it, I'm going to whack you if you start that. Now go in and brush your teeth."

He gave her a dirty look, but he went. She sat down at the table. "How come you were late for supper?"

I didn't want to go into the whole story, and besides Dad was sitting in the next room. "We had a lot of late business," I said.

"We saved you some beans. There were lots left over."

"They were good, Sally," I said.

"I guess everybody's getting tired of beans," she said. She looked kind of sad.

"I'm not tired of beans," I said. "I love beans."

"You're just saying that," she said.

Luckily Dad came into the kitchen right then. He didn't sit down but stood in the door. I knew what he was going to say. He'd gotten the idea that it was his job to bawl Sally out, not mine. "Sally," he said, "what's this idea that you kids are going to be farmed out to live with relatives?"

She kind of blushed. "What?" she said.

"You know what I'm talking about."

"The baby overheard you and Margene talking," I said.

"Oh," she said.

"Now look," he said. "I want everybody in this family to stop all this gloom and doom stuff. I know times are hard, but we'll manage. Is that understood?"

We hung our heads down. "Yes," I said.

"Yes," Sally said.

He came over to the table and patted Sally on the head the way he did, and then gave my shoulder a squeeze. He pulled out a chair, sat down with us, leaned back, and patted his round belly. "Actually we're bound for an upturn. I've got a new plan. I'm going down to New York in a day or so and start scouting around down there. There's bound to be something for me. I'd have gone with one of the swing bands long ago except that I've been stuck up here and everybody's forgotten about me. If I'd been in New York, or even Chi or L.A., I'd have been getting calls right and left. In the old days everybody knew me. They'd say, if you want a real pro who can cut anything, get Warren Lundquist. They all wanted me to go with them — Goldkette, Whiteman, the Casa Loma bunch, you name it. But I had a family and your mother didn't want me to go on the road, she wanted me here. I didn't blame her — you need a man at home when you're raising kids. So I stayed and now the business around here has dried up. I've got to get my name back in circulation again. Once I get playing around a little, people will know about it. They'll say, Warren Lundquist is playing again. Everybody'll want me. Of course it'll mean my being away two or three days at a time. But you kids can manage by yourselves for a day or so."

"Dad — "

"So when you look at it that way, losing the Elks Club job was a blessing in disguise."

We stared at him. "You mean the Elks Club job is finished for good?"

"Didn't I tell you? Oh, I thought I did. No, they have to cut down on expenses. They're cutting the band down to a trio — trumpet, piano, and drums. Me and the base player are out. But as I say, it's a blessing in disguise. I'll get the New York thing going and we'll be in clover. Oh, it's bound to be slow at first, but once people hear me again, it'll pick up fast. And then what we'll do is get a nice apartment in New York, some nice place on the East Side or maybe down in the Village, and move down. How'd you kids like to live in New York? It's a great town, a whole lot better than being stuck up here in the sticks all your life."

"Dad, maybe in the meantime you could get a day job."

He banged his hand down on the table. "Don't bring that up anymore."

I sure didn't want to get him sore again. But I tried to keep up my courage to argue with him. "Dad, just for a year. Until times get better. Until they reopen the country club. You keep saying they're going to do that any day now."

"Jack, I'm not going through this with you again."

"But, Dad, only for a little — "

"God damn it, no," he shouted. "That's final." He stood up and stomped out of the room, and in a moment I heard the door slam.

"See what you did, Jack?"

"He's going down to the Colonial," I said.

"Why do you always have to make him mad?"
She was mad herself.

"What are you yelling at me for, I was just trying
to help."

"Don't shout at me, Jack."

"I wasn't shouting."

"Yes you are," she shouted.

I stopped. "Let's not fight, Sal. I'm tired of fight-
ing."

She bent her head down. Neither of us said anything for a minute. Then I said, "Maybe I could quit
school in the fall and get a regular job."

"You can't, you're not old enough to get working
papers."

"Well, maybe I could get some kind of job anyway."

"By that time Henry will be out in Chicago and I'll
be down in New Orleans," she said. "God, that'll be
awful living with them down there."

"I think Henry's got it worse. I don't think
Grandma and Grandpa would be as strict as Uncle
Edgar and Aunt Mabel," I said.

"Well, anyway."

We sat there thinking for a minute. Then I said,
"If only we could get a lot of money. If only there
was some way." I gave her a little look. "I mean
suppose some rich guy dropped a huge wad of
money out of his pocket and I found it."

"You'd have to turn it back."

"But suppose I didn't?"

"You'd get caught, anyway," she said. "They'd
make you give it back."

"But suppose. Suppose I happened to look in the back of this car and there was a briefcase jammed up with money that he was taking to some big deal somewhere."

"That'd be stealing," she said.

"Well so what?" I said. "I mean a guy that rich wouldn't miss it."

She looked worried. "You wouldn't really steal money, would you, Jack?"

"Why not?" I heard.

Then we heard a noise and realized that the baby was standing by the door. "You've been listening in," I shouted.

"Honest, Jack," he said. "I didn't hear anything about stealing."

We broke up laughing, Sally and me. Henry couldn't figure out what we were laughing about, and he stood there staring and shouting, "What are you laughing about, what are you laughing about?" But we couldn't tell him, we just went on laughing and collapsing in our chairs, so finally he got mad and stomped off. After a while we stopped laughing and Sally put Henry to bed and then we went to bed, too. And as I lay there waiting to go to sleep, I realized I'd made a mistake bringing it up about stealing with Sally. Now half the family knew, and pretty soon Dad would know, too, because Henry would say something about it if he didn't forget.

When I got up in the morning I was faced with another problem — the cut on my hand. I didn't want Mr. Slater to see it, that was for sure. I went into the bathroom, stripped off the bandage, and had a look at it. It had stopped bleeding, and when I washed the dried blood away I could see that it had begun to close up. It really wasn't much of a cut; I'd had plenty of cuts like it before. But I knew that if I bumped against something it might start bleeding again — it might start bleeding again anyway, just from not having the bandage on.

But I couldn't leave the bandage on. So I made my sandwiches, left the house, and hitched out to the boat club. It had cleared off during the night. The sun was up over the hills to the east of the lake, the sky was bright blue, and there was a light breeze blowing. It was going to be beautiful down at the boat club. If the wind picked up any at all, it'd be a perfect day for racing. We were going to have a busy day.

As I came through the iron gates I had a quick look at them for signs of blood. There weren't any that I could see, but it was hard to tell with a quick glance. I walked down the driveway smelling the pines in the breeze and feeling nervous about being able to put on a good act when Mr. Slater told me somebody had broken in. I kept my left hand in my pocket and tried to look casual. As I came up to the parking lot at the back of the clubhouse, I saw that there was a police car there already. I stopped and swallowed; and then I went on up to the clubhouse and in the back door. Mr. Slater was in the storeroom with two cops, talking. I stood at the door.

"It looks like vandalism," one of the cops was saying.

"I cahn't tell until we check it. 'Oo knows what thyve tyken."

"What happened?" I said.

"Somebody broke in agine last night."

"Did they take anything?" I said.

"I don't know as yet," Mr. Slater said. "Jack, get a broom and dustpan and clean up this bloody glass before somebody gets cut."

"Okay," I said. I went out and got a broom and dustpan. There was no way I could sweep with one hand. I just prayed that the cut wouldn't open up. One of the cops was examining the window. "There's a couple of bloody fingerprints here," he said.

"You ain't gonna fingerprint every kid in Stevens-town."

I stood there with the broom and dustpan in one hand, still keeping the other hand in my pocket, waiting until the cop got out of the way. Finally he did. I set the dustpan down on the floor and began sweeping up the broken glass. The cop began to scratch his head. "That's funny," he said. "Most of the glass is outside there on the gravel. Like some-body broke the window from the inside." My skin grew cold and my heart raced.

The other cop shrugged. "Some of the pieces were bound to fall outside. Besides, they probably pulled the jagged pieces out by hand and laid them down on the gravel to cut down on the noise."

"It still don't make no sense. It looks like it was busted from the inside."

"How could that be?" Mr. Slater said.

The cop looked at him. "You sure you locked up good?"

Mr. Slater was getting cross. "Of course I'm sure."

"And there wasn't nobody in here when you locked up?"

Mr. Slater gestured around. "Where in bloody 'ell could anybody 'ide in 'ere?"

Everybody looked around. Of course when Mr.

Slater had locked up I'd been hiding behind the stack of soda pop cases. But now the stack was down and scattered all around. There didn't seem like any place where a person could hide. "That's true," the cop said. "You sure you got a good look inside?"

" 'Ow much of a look would it 'ave tyken?" Mr. Slater snapped. He was pretty annoyed that they didn't believe him.

I went on sweeping, trying to get the glass up as quickly as possible so nobody would notice how much there was. I swept it into a little pile and then stooped down to sweep it into the dustpan. I slid my hand down the broom, and suddenly I felt a quick sting, and I knew that I had opened up the cut again. I clenched my hand tight around the broom handle to keep the blood from flowing and quickly swept the glass into the dustpan. Then I stood up, still with my hand clenched around the broom and headed out of the room. I was almost at the door when Mr. Slater called, "Jack."

I turned around.

"Jack, you're bleeding."

I unwrapped my hand from the broom and stared at it. The cut was oozing blood.

"You must 'ave cut yourself picking up that glass. That wasn't very bright, was it? God, what a morning. All right, get rid of that glass and go get the first-aid kit out of my office and put something on it." He sighed. "What a mess."

I had gotten away with it by the skin of my teeth. The luckiest part of it was taking down that stack of soda pop cases, so that it didn't seem possible for anybody to hide in there. The cops might have thought Mr. Slater had been careless about locking up, but he sure didn't, and he was the important one. The whole thing had been sort of unusual. It just never occurred to anybody that I would get myself locked into the storeroom.

Mr. Slater had me straighten out the storeroom from where I'd messed it up and told me to count the cases to see what was missing. Of course nothing was missing, but I put a bunch of bottles of soda in the cooler and told him that about six were gone. He said, "Just some kids fooling around." In the afternoon a man came out from the hardware store to glaze the window, and that was that. But for the rest of the day I made sure I did a perfect job on everything, just in case.

The one thing left over out of it all was that now I knew that Mr. Slater had a lot of money hidden in his sleeping bag. It wasn't too unusual for somebody to take kickbacks. I don't mean that everybody did; there were lots of honest people running clubs; but a lot of people did take them, and with times as hard as they were, you just had to go along with it if you wanted the work. When it came to the salesmen, Mr. Slater had the upper hand. There were plenty of liquor wholesalers he could buy from; either they kicked back or he'd buy his stuff from somebody else. I didn't know how much money Mr. Slater made. I figured that it must be a pretty good salary — probably seventy-five a week or maybe even more. That fancy place where he worked in the winter was so full of millionaires, according to him, they could pay him almost anything and not miss it. But my guess was that he was pulling down another hundred a month in kickbacks. There would be the liquor salesman, and the soda pop guy, and the guy who supplied the peanuts and potato chips, and the restaurant supply house that sold us glassware and ashtrays and stuff. Then there was all that boating equipment. Of course the club members generally bought what they needed for their boats themselves, but Mr. Slater kept a certain amount of stuff on hand — deck paint, brushes, oarlocks, and other fittings. We had a gas pump, too. And of course there was the stuff that we bought to keep the clubhouse and the grounds in shape — gravel for the driveway, and lawnmowers, and lumber and such for dock repairs. Oh, there was plenty of money flowing around Mr. Slater, and he was finding ways to scoop some of it. It was my guess that it wasn't just kickbacks, either. Each member of the club paid in a hundred dollars a year in dues, which is why you had to be rich to belong to it. Mr. Slater kept the books on all this money. I didn't know much about bookkeeping, but I'd read about people who cheated on their accounts. What you did was put down that you'd spent twenty dollars for paint, when you'd only spent ten, and you'd keep the extra ten yourself. I guess it was probably more complicated than that, but I knew you could do it. And if you could, I figured Mr. Slater would.

What was I going to do about it? The honest thing would be to tell somebody on the members' committee that Mr. Slater was taking kickbacks. But I knew that wouldn't do any good. They wouldn't believe me; or if they did, Mr. Slater would say that I was a liar and then he'd fire me. That was all I could get out of being honest — getting fired.

I still hadn't decided what I ought to do with the ten dollars reward I got from Mr. Waterman. I wanted a new glove, all right. Why was it up to me to worry about Sally's new outfit? That was Dad's job, not mine. But I couldn't help worrying about it. What I kept hoping was that one day he'd come home and say, "Well, I have enough dough for Sal's outfit," and then I wouldn't have to think about it anymore. I hoped he would remember; I didn't want to keep reminding him. I didn't want to keep reminding him about stuff. I figured he was doing the best he could; he had a lot of things to worry about and it wasn't surprising if he forgot little things like milk every once in a while. I just hoped he remembered about Sal's outfit, though.

Sometimes things got him down, too. He always tried to be cheerful, but there were times when I could tell he wasn't feeling too good. For example, a couple of days after I got locked in the storeroom, I came home from Charlie's around supper time, and he was sitting in the kitchen all by himself with no lights on, smoking. I could tell from the cigarette butts in the ashtray that he'd been sitting there for a long time, thinking and smoking and not noticing that it was getting dark. "Can I turn on the light?" I said.

"Oh? Jack? Yeah, sure, turn it on. I didn't realize it was so dark."

It worried me a little to find him sitting in the dark, because that's what Mom did before she went nuts. "Do you feel okay?"

"Oh yeah, sure," he said. "I'm all right. I was just thinking."

"Is something wrong?"

He shrugged. "No. Nothing special. I guess I've just got the blues. Worrying about work all the time

90

and where the money's going to come from — it gets to me sometimes. I'll be all right."

"You want me to start supper?"

"Supper? Oh, right. Sal's eating over at Margene's tonight. I told her we'd take care of ourselves." Suddenly he jumped up and clapped his hands. "No sense in glooming over things that can't be helped. Let's look on the bright side." He clapped his hands again, and began to sing: "Happy days are heeeere again, the skies above are cleeeear again." He stopped singing. "Where's Henry?"

"He's probably out back."

"Okay, men's night out," he said. "When you're feeling blue the best thing is a feast." He reached in his pocket and pulled out a handful of change. "Almost a dollar," he said. "What have we got to eat around here?" He began slamming open the cupboards and rummaging around in the shelves. "Here's some spuds," he said. "And a couple of onions. That'll do for a start. Get Henry in from the outside and you two guys start peeling them. I'm going over to the store. I'll be right back."

It made me happy to see him in a good mood again. I went out to the back, where Henry was drawing on the sidewalk with a piece of chalk. "Hey Henry, come in, we're making a feast."

"Who's making a feast?"

"Me and Dad. You can be in on it, too."

He put the chalk in his pocket. "Okay," he said.

We went in and I started him off peeling the potatoes. "Don't peel them too thick," I said. "That's all we've got."

"Why do I have to peel the potatoes?" he said.

"Would you rather peel the onions?"

"No."

"Well, then," I said.

"I wouldn't rather do either," he said. "I'd rather watch you."

"Ho, ho, ho," I said. "Don't you want to be in on it?"

"Yes," he said.

"Then shut up and peel."

So he did; and about the time we were getting finished Dad walked back in with a bag of groceries. He set it down on the kitchen table. "My boys," he said, "Lafayette has arrived." He began taking stuff out of the bag. "Two pounds top round, ground lean." He put it on the table. "Three tomatoes, hothouse, not quite ripe." He put them on the table. "One Mrs. Frisbee's apple pie." He put the pie on the table. "And last but not least, one mild Havana cigar, five cents." He rubbed his hands. "Let's go."

So Henry and I sat at the table and watched him cook and kidded him when he spilled stuff. He fried the potatoes and onions, and broiled the hamburgers, and served it hot, and boy was it good after the beans and franks we'd been living off. Then we ate the pie, and afterwards Henry and I did the dishes, and Dad sat in the kitchen with us drinking coffee and smoking his cigar and telling music business stories. Then Sally came home, and Dad said that now we had enough for Monopoly, so we got the set out.

"The flatiron is missing," Dad said.

"I know," Sally said. "Henry lost it."

"I did —"

"Sssssshush," Dad said. "Nobody lost it — the fairies took it."

"I guess the fairies took the other dice," I said.

"It doesn't matter." Dad said, "We'll just throw the same one twice." Carefully he snubbed out the cigar. "Just enough left for a few puffs before bed," he said. "Who goes first? Hap-py days are heeeere again. . . ."

The next morning I walked around to Charlie Franks' house, which is what I generally did on school days. It wasn't exactly on the way to school, but it wasn't too far out of the way, either, and it was more fun to walk to school with your friend than to go by yourself. Besides, it gave me a chance to think about whether I was going to spend the ten dollars reward Mr. Waterman had given me for turning in his wallet for a baseball glove or save it, just in case Dad didn't have the money for Sally's new outfit. I sure didn't want to spend it for that, though.

Charlie's father was a mechanic at Dubrow's garage. He made a good salary and they lived in a pretty nice two-family house, with furniture that wasn't all messed up like ours was and enough bedrooms so Charlie and his sister each had their own rooms. I spent a lot of time up at Charlie's, fooling around in his room. He had his own radio, a Philco table model. Practically every night before supper we'd listen. We usually would hear "Tom Mix" and "Jack Armstrong" and "Bobby Benson" and "The H Bar O Ranch." They were fifteen minutes each, so you could always get in three or four before supper time. We tried not to miss any episodes, but it didn't matter much if you did — you usually could figure out what had happened. I would have liked to have Charlie come down to my house sometimes, too, but the truth was, I was ashamed that I didn't have a room of my own for us to fool around in. Besides, we didn't have a radio.

School didn't start until quarter of nine, but with Charlie you had to allow plenty of time. When I got there, as usual, he wasn't ready. His mother was in the kitchen washing the breakfast dishes. "He can't find his history book," she said. "You better go up there and help him find it, Jack, or you'll never get to school."

I went up to Charlie's room. It was a terrible mess, the way it always was. His clothes were hanging all over the chairs, and the floor was covered with parts from a clock and his baseball glove and a lot of comic books with their covers scuffled off. "If you cleaned up some of this junk," I said, "maybe you could find something every once in a while."

"Naw," he said. "I like it this way. If I put stuff away, I forget when I put it and then I never can find it again. But if I just throw it around, it stays in plain sight so I can find it."

"Then how come you can't find your history book?"

"Somebody must have shoved it under something."

"If you'd have done your homework over the weekend, it might not be underneath everything."

"You're nobody to talk about doing homework."

"I don't have to do any homework because I'm so smart," I said.

"Yeah, sure, Jack. Help me find my history book or we'll be late."

So I looked under the bed and there it was, and we got organized and started off for school. "Listen, Jack, what about going to Boston to see the Yanks?"

"I think I shouldn't spend my ten dollars."

"Aw come on, Jack, what are you going to save it for?"

I didn't want to tell him the truth. I was sort of ashamed of Dad and being poor and all. I mean everybody said there was nothing to be ashamed of being poor in these times, but I felt ashamed of it anyway — ashamed of having old broken-down furniture and having to sleep in the living room. And I was sort of ashamed of Dad for not taking a day job and for putting himself first over his own family, the way he did a lot. So I didn't really want to talk to Charlie about it; but I had to give him some explanation that would make sense. "Well, the thing is, Dad's planning to go down to New York for a few days to look for some gigs down there, and I figure I ought to have a little money for emergencies while he's gone."

"Get him to leave you some money," Charlie said.

I didn't want to say anything, but I had to. "Well, we don't have too much money."

"No, but I mean he could easily leave you ten, couldn't he? He's got that much money, hasn't he?"

I didn't say anything. Then I said, "Oh well, sure. Sure, he's got that much money."

"Well, then, we can go."

I felt sort of down. It made me feel lousy to be so poor and have to lie about it to my friend. But I just wasn't going to admit to Charlie how poor we really were. We walked along not saying anything for a minute and gradually I began to get sore at Dad. Why did I have to lie to my friend just because Dad didn't want to be realistic? Why did I have to worry about Sally's outfit or whether we had enough milk just because he didn't want to have a day job? What was terrible about that? I had a day job, didn't I? Suddenly I blurted out, "Okay, the hell with my father. Let's go."

We worked up our plans. We decided to go on Wednesday because it was a doubleheader. We would hitch to Boston in the morning. Even if we had bad luck getting rides, we'd still be there in plenty of time to buy a glove before we went out to the ball game.

On Wednesday morning I told Sally I was having supper over at Charlie's and not to worry if I didn't get home until late. Then I went over there. For once he hadn't lost anything and he was ready to go. He told his mother that he was having supper at my house; we were going to do our history together, which ought to have made her suspicious, but it didn't. Then we took off. We were pretty nervous about getting caught. We started off in the direction of school, but as soon as we were out of sight of Charlie's house we swung onto a back street so as to cut around town toward the highway. Once we met a bunch of guys from our class heading for school. "Hey, you guys are going in the wrong direction," they shouted. We grinned, but we didn't say anything.

We swung around town, picked up Route 12, which went north to Route 20, the main route into Boston. We got a lift right away. I sort of recognized the guy. He said, "Aren't you Warren Lundquist's kid?"

"Yes," I said.

"How come you kids aren't in school?"

"They're having a teacher's meeting in our class, today," Charlie said.

"Humph," he said. "When I was a kid, if you had a day off from school you worked."

We didn't have any answer to that. He dropped us off at Route 20, and pretty soon we got a lift to Boston. I was feeling sort of excited and good. We'd escaped, and there wasn't anybody who could tell us what to do all day long. I felt in my back pocket for the ten. It was still there.

We got to Boston by eleven o'clock. I had ripped out an ad from the paper for a sporting goods store, which had the address on it. We didn't know anything about Boston, and it took us a while to figure out how to get to the store. But finally somebody told us which streetcar to take. I tell you, just walking into that store made me all excited. The whole place was filled with the smell of leather. It really got me, that smell. We had plenty of time, so first we wandered all around, looking at the golf clubs and tennis stuff and archery sets. They even had a few footballs out, although it wasn't the football season. After we'd killed a half an hour we went over to the base-ball glove section. There they were — I don't know how many, dozens of them. Some of them were stuck up on little stands. Others were lying flat in the racks. They were all different colors: yellow, red, brown, and real dark brown. Oh, they looked good. It made me feel rich just to see them all.

The first thing we did was to check out the prices. They had some real expensive ones — there was a big catcher's mitt that was nine dollars and ninety-five cents. The first baseman's mitts were pretty expensive, too. But there were plenty of fielder's gloves for around five or six or seven dollars, and we began trying on some of these. Of course Charlie kept trying on ones, too, even though he wasn't going to buy one. And of course right away a salesman came over. Naturally he thought we were trying to steal something.

"Can I help you, sonny?" he said.

"We want to buy a glove," I said. "But first we want to try some on."

"Those gloves will run you six or seven dollars, sonny."

"I've got ten dollars," I said. I took out the bill and showed it to him. I didn't want to get into a rush; I wanted to take plenty of time. "We want to try some, first."

"All right, sonny," he said. "Take your time." I put the bill back in my pocket, and he went away, but I noticed that he stood about two counters away from us, with his arms folded over his chest, and glanced over at us about every minute. Still, I wasn't going to be rushed. In buying a baseball glove there were a lot of things to check out. Of course you wanted it to be good and sturdy, so the stuffing doesn't start leaking out around the lacing. Then it should have a good deep pocket. You had to build up the pocket yourself by using it — some guys tied a ball into it and left it like that for a few days, but that never worked too well for me. So you wanted to make sure the pocket was right. Then of course it should feel right. I mean it should fit just comfortable with the pocket exactly at the place where your thumb and forefinger meet. There were a lot of things to worry about, which is why I didn't want to be rushed.

Naturally, Charlie had a lot of opinions about it, but being a left-hander he couldn't get a feel of the ones I was looking over. I guess I must have tried on about twenty. Finally I narrowed it down to a dark leather Charlie Gehringer model, with crisscross webbing; a light-colored Mule Haas model; and a Joe Cronin model, which was kind of reddish. I'll admit it, I wasn't crazy about the Joe Cronin model, but he was my favorite player — shortstop for the Red Sox.

"I'd like to get the Joe Cronin." I said, "but it doesn't feel too good."

"Maybe you could break it in," Charlie said.

"I'm worried about that. I mean spending all that money and maybe it would never feel right."

"I guess you shouldn't get it," Charlie said.

"So it's between the Gehringer and the Mule Haas." I tried them both again and still I couldn't decide. "I wish we could have a few catches."

"They won't let you do that in a store," Charlie said.

"I'd like to, though. I can't decide."

"Flip a coin."

"I don't want to do that." I tried them both again, pounding the pockets with my fist to imitate the feeling of catching a ball. "All right. The Gehringer," I said. I put the Mule Haas back on its stand, and the minute I did I began to worry if I'd made the right choice. I took it off again and tried it. "Maybe the Mule Haas is better," I said.

"God, make up your mind."

I tried them both again. "No, the Gehringer." So I took it over to the salesman and bought it. It cost six dollars and ninety-five cents, which was a pretty good amount of money for a glove, but it was worth it. The salesman put it in a box and wrapped it up with string and brown paper, and we went outside. But I couldn't stand not looking at my new glove, so I busted the string off the box, took the glove out, and threw the wrapping and the box in a trash basket. Then I undid my belt and put it through the glove strap and let the glove hang from my waist. "Nobody will be able to steal it at the ball game if I carry it on my belt," I said. But that wasn't the real reason. The real reason why I put it on my belt was because it made me feel proud to walk around wearing it that way.

Then we asked somebody which streetcar to take to Fenway and went out there. We were way early, but we didn't mind, we liked to watch them take batting practice. The Red Sox split the doubleheader. In the first game Jimmy Foxx hit two homers and Gehrig hit one, and the Sox won six to four. In the second game everything went wrong: the Red Sox gave up five runs in the second inning and lost nine to six. But we didn't mind. A good hitting game is great to watch.

6

On Thursday afternoon Charlie and I got kicked off the baseball team for playing hooky. What happened was this. On Thursday, we forged notes from our parents saying that we had been sick on Wednesday — you know, the usual kind of note that says, "Jack was absent from school on Wednesday because he had a cold, very truly yours, Warren Lundquist." The trouble was, it made our teacher suspicious that me and Charlie were both sick on the same day, being as we were friends. So the secretary from the office called up our parents. Dad wasn't home, but Mrs. Franks was, and she hit the roof. So they called us into the office and gave us hell, and then they put us on detention — an hour after school every day for a month. That worried us a lot, because it would mean that we would be late for baseball practice every day. But we needn't have worried about it, because when we went out to practice that afternoon,

101

Coach Gans came over to us and said, "Franks, you and Lundquist turn in your uniforms."

We stood there in front of him not believing what he was saying. "But, Coach," Charlie said.

"Turn them in," he said. Then he walked away. I looked at Charlie and he looked at me, and then we walked into the locker room, took off our uniforms, put on our regular clothes, and walked home. We didn't talk much. I was having trouble keeping from crying, and I was afraid that if I said anything I would bust out with it. Charlie cursed out Gans a few times, but they were pretty feeble curses and I knew he was feeling terrible, too. Finally I got home. I went into Sally's room and lay down on her bed, and the tears started to leak out of my eyes, and suddenly I was sitting up on the bed, mad and crying and sticking my fists into my eyes to stop the tears from coming. Then I heard somebody slam the back door and I stopped crying and tried to wipe my face.

Sally came in. "What's the matter?" she said.

"Nothing," I said.

"You were crying," she said.

"No I wasn't," I said. "I got kicked off the baseball team."

"What for?"

So I told her, and I began to feel a little better talking about it, but not much, for when I went out into the living room there was that mitt sitting there on top of Dad's record cabinet. All of a sudden I hated it; I didn't know if I'd ever want to use it. I'd never caught a ball with it, and I didn't know if I ever would. Oh, I tried to tell myself that it didn't matter, that I'd be able to go out for the team the next year, that I might not have made the team anyway, and so forth. But it didn't do any good. I just felt sick about it. And making it worse was that something else came to me. That was the idea that I'd done exactly what I blamed Dad for doing all the time. I'd gone out and been irresponsible, just because I wanted to, without thinking about Sally's new outfit or anything else. In a way, it served me right; but that didn't make me feel any better.

On Saturday something happened down at the boat club that took my mind off it a little. Mr. Waterman, the guy whose wallet I'd found, came over to me when I was mopping the place out that morning. He stood with his hands in his pockets watching me for a minute. I glanced at him, but went on working, trying to make it look like I was doing a good job. Finally he said, "Your name's Jack, isn't it?"

I stopped mopping. "Yes, sir," I said.

"Jack what?"

"Jack Lundquist."

He stared at me for another moment. Then he said, "Listen, Jack, I'm having some people for cocktails next Sunday afternoon. I need a bartender. Think you could handle it?"

"I think so, sir," I said. "But I'll have to see if Mr. Slater will let me off."

He stared at me for another minute. "He'll let you off," he said. "Just tell him I said I needed you."

I didn't think Mr. Slater was going to like being told what to do very much, but I wanted the job and besides, there wasn't any way around it. So I waited until I had finished the mopping and then I went into Mr. Slater's office. "Mr. Slater, Mr. Waterman asked me if I could handle a cocktail party for him next Sunday. I said I would have to ask you."

"Mr. Waterman?" He looked at me. "What sort of party did 'e say?"

"A cocktail party. He didn't tell me much about it."

He frowned. "I suppose it's because of the wallet — 'e wanted to do you a good turn." He thumped on the desk with a pencil. "I cahn't very well spare you, Jack," he said.

"I'll tell Mr. Waterman — "

"No, no," he said quickly. "That's all roight, I'll get along. You go ahead and do it."

I found Mr. Waterman out on the dock looking over his boat. "Mr. Slater said it would be all right."

"I thought he would," he said. "I'll send somebody down for you in the station wagon. Be ready at three o'clock. Bring your mess jacket. Also, we're going to borrow glassware from the club. Pack up three dozen each highballs and lowballs. There should be liquor cartons around to pack them in."

"Three dozen each."

"Right," he said. Then he turned away and back to looking over his boat.

I was pretty excited. It was just what I had been hoping would happen. If I began getting jobs at private houses, I could really pick up a lot of extra money. Of course I didn't really know how to run a cocktail party — it made me nervous to think about it. But I figured I could work it out. I'd got pretty good at making drinks. There were a lot of fancy ones in the bartender's guide Mr. Slater had under the bar that I didn't know how to make. But I could make all the regular ones — manhattans, martinis, old-fashioneds, Tom Collinses, bronxes, whiskey sours — those were the main ones besides ordinary highballs. It would be terrific experience. I figured that if I kept on getting experience at bartending, I'd always have a way of making money. It was a lot easier life than working in the mill, that was for sure.

Anyway, it gave me a new daydream, which I worked up while I was picking up the parking lot that afternoon:

I'm standing in Mr. Waterman's party, tending bar. The place is filled with fifty millionaires. I'm whipping out their drinks and saying, "Yes, sir," and "No, sir," and after a while these two millionaires are standing there near the bar, and one of them says to the other, "The Red Sox can't win with a second baseman who only hits .250." And the other millionaire says, "Melillo hit more than that. He hit up around .290." "No," the first millionaire says, "he hit .250." And the second millionaire says, "I'll bet you a thousand he didn't hit .250." And then I say, "Excuse me, sir, I don't mean to butt in, but I wouldn't make that bet if I were you." So the millionaire looks at me, sort of frowning, and then he says, "Are you sure?" So I say, "Sure, he usually hits around .250 He hit .226 last year and .261 the year before and he's hitting .250 now." So both millionaires stare at me, and then the second one says, "You have a pretty good head for figures, son." He reaches into his pocket and takes out a card. "Here," he says, "give me a call at that number on Monday. I could use a bright kid like you."

That was as far as I got before I had to go in and start working the bar.

It was already early in May. School would be out

in six weeks. I could hardly wait for it to end. If I'd have been on the baseball team I wouldn't have minded if school went on all summer, but now I couldn't stand it. I hardly did any studying — all I wanted to do was get it over with. Mr. Slater hadn't said anything about working at the boat club full time over the summer, but I was pretty sure he was going to. In the spring, the only people using the club were the ones who lived around Stevenstown, or at least in this part of Massachusetts. When summer came and school let out, a lot of people from New York and Boston would come down and open up their summer houses, and they'd be around the boat club a lot during the day. Mr. Slater said that there would be sailing and swimming classes, as well as tennis lessons. There would be plenty to do, and I knew he'd need somebody to help him.

So I was just waiting everything out. And then on Wednesday night when we were having dinner, Dad told us that he was going down to New York for a couple of days. Sally was learning how to make fried chicken, which was cheap. She had cooked some for supper. She hadn't cooked it long enough and it was pretty raw, but we were all pretending it was delicious so as not to discourage her.

"Very good, Sally," Dad said.

"Terrific, Sal," I said.

"It isn't cooked enough," she said.

"Sure it is," Dad said. "Oh, it could have been done a hair more but it's fine anyway."

"I don't think it's cooked enough," she said.

"It's terrific, Sally," I said.

"It's terrific, Sally," the baby said.

"Maybe I just got a bad piece," she said.

There was a little silence and then Dad said, "Well kids, I'm going down to New York tomorrow."

None of us said anything. Then I said, "For how long?"

"A couple of days," he said. "I just want to look up some people I know and see what's going on."

"Are you going to have gigs in New York, Daddy?" the baby said.

"That's the idea," he said. "This time of year I should be able to pick up a lot of work right away." The idea was that in May and June you got a lot of weddings and socialite parties, besides the high school and college proms. The proms were especially good because the college students usually got drunk and wanted the band to play overtime, which meant extra pay. You could make fifty dollars on a good weekend. Of course Dad had a handicap, because there wasn't nearly as much call for trombones as for some of the other instruments. The pianists got the most work — there was always a piano player on every gig, sometimes just him alone. Drummers got the next most work, and then guitarists and bassists. On a lot of gigs they'd just have a pianist plus a couple of rhythm players — maybe bass and drums or drums and guitar. Next came trumpet and saxophone players. There were a lot of little trios and quartets that would use one or two horns. If there was just one horn it'd be a trumpet or alto saxophone, because they wanted one of the higher instruments for the melody. If it was two horns it might be trumpet and trombone, but usually it would be trumpet and alto saxophone. Even with a five or six-piece band using three horns, they wouldn't necessarily use a trombone player; it might be trumpet and two saxes. Only when you got into the seven or eight-piece groups or bigger, would they normally have a trombone. Dad complained about it a lot. "I can get up into the alto range all right," he would say. "Dave and I never had any trouble making it work with alto and trombone. Leaders shouldn't be so conservative." But there was no use complaining about it.

Anyway, no matter what kind of work there was going, you had to be there to get it. In the music business, the best-known players — known among musicians, I mean — usually got more calls for work than they could do. They would have friends who they would turn their extra work over to. Say one guy was playing in a pit band in a theater and he got a call for a real high-paying dance job; he'd get somebody he knew to substitute for him in the pit band so he could play his dance job. Then someday the other guy would get him a job substituting. Every musician had certain guys who he called first to cover for him. The idea was if Dad got down to New York and met some people, they'd start calling him to sub, and then after awhile the bookers and the leaders would get to know him, and they'd start calling him directly for work. A good player could get a lot of work. In June, with so many weddings and proms, a guy could end up with three jobs in one day. He might have a wedding reception at noon, a cocktail party at five o'clock, and then a prom at night. But you had to be there.

"How long are you going to be down there?" Sally asked.

"I'm coming back on Friday," he said.

I knew he wouldn't, but I didn't say anything.

"Now I want you all to look after each other. I want somebody to make sure that the bab — Henry gets to bed on time. You'll have to see that he's properly dressed for school."

"I can look after myself," the baby said. "I don't need anybody to boss me."

"Don't start an argument with me, Henry," Dad said. "Just do as you're told. Sally, you see that he gets going in the morning."

"Okay," she said. "See that, Henry, you're supposed to obey me."

He stuck out his lower lip at her, but he didn't say anything.

"Yes," Dad said, "things are looking up. A couple of good gigs will turn everything around. Once my name gets around I'll have plenty of work, and we'll think about moving down to New York. Maybe get a nice house in the suburbs, up there in Westchester or over in Jersey. Someplace like Scarsdale or Greenwich. You ought to see those places, one big fancy place after another. Sal, how'd you like to live in a place like that, where half the people have butlers and chauffeurs?"

"Listen, Dad," Sally said, "do you think if you got a good gig, we could get my new outfit? The play is pretty soon."

"What?" he said. "The new outfit? Oh yes," he said.

"Well, Sal," I said, "Dad's got a lot of things to spend money on."

"No, no, we'll definitely get it as soon as I get back. Maybe Saturday morning. All I need is one good gig, and I'm bound to get that. At this time of year I can't miss."

I just wished he would stop making these promises. Of course maybe he would get some gigs; and if Sally grabbed him right away before the bill collectors caught up with him, or he'd spent the money some other way, she could probably get her new outfit. But was it really true that he couldn't miss getting a gig, or was it just some more of his dreaming? I didn't know.

In the meanwhile I had other things to worry about. To tell the truth, I was getting pretty nervous about the bartending job at Mr. Waterman's. What if a lot of people began asking for funny drinks I'd never heard of? I figured that all I had to do was to stand behind a table or something and mix drinks; but what if I was supposed to go around serving them? I decided I ought to bone up a little, so I went around to the public library and looked for a book on bartending. They didn't have exactly that, but they had a book on how to give parties, which had a list of cocktail recipes in the back, and I made myself memorize three of them every night.

On Sunday I thought about bringing the book with me, but I decided against it. It would make me look like I didn't know what I was doing, which I didn't want, even if it was true. Besides, the book might get something spilled on it, and then I would have to pay for it. So I didn't bring it.

As soon as the noontime bar rush was over, I began packing glasses into liquor cartons I'd saved. Mr. Slater grumbled about that. He said how could he run the bar if I was taking all the glasses away? But he was only saying that, because we had plenty. Besides, he didn't want to cross Mr. Waterman. At three o'clock I went out into the parking lot to wait, and in a few minutes a station wagon showed up. It was a brand-new Buick, all shiny and beautiful. There was a chauffeur driving it, wearing a cap and uniform. It made me excited just to see it.

"You the bartender?" the chauffeur said.

"Yes," I said.

"You ain't nothin' but a kid," he said.

"I'm sixteen," I said, which was a lie.

"Okay, throw your stuff in the back."

I went around to the back of the station wagon. It took me a minute to figure out how to open it, but I got the stuff in. I didn't know where I was supposed to ride. I figured that the chauffeur wouldn't want me riding next to him, so I started opening the door to the middle seat. "You ain't gentry," he said. "You ride up here with me." I got in next to him and we drove away. I must say, I felt pretty snazzy crunching down the driveway in that big new car.

The Watermans' house was around the other side of the lake from the boat club. It was really something. There was an iron fence along the front and big bushes and shrubs along the fence so riff-raff couldn't see in. There were two huge stone pillars on either side of the gate and then a long bluestone driveway sort of winding through the lawn, which was filled with big old trees. The house was made of blocks of gray stone, big and heavy and sort of looming up out of the lawn like a great rock. We drove on around behind the house. There was a green painted wooden six-car garage with two other cars in it, a Cadillac and a Pontiac roadster. The lawn sloped down from the house to the lake, where there was a boat house and a dock with a big Gar Wood tied up to it. It was just beautiful seeing the lawn all dappled

111

with the sun coming through the trees and the lake at the end of it. I knew it must be terrific to be rich and wake up in the morning and look out the window and see the lawn and the lake.

In the middle of the lawn they'd set up a tent roof. There was a table under it covered with a white tablecloth. "There's your bar," the chauffeur said. "Get your glasses, set up, and then come on up to the kitchen and I'll show you where your liquor is."

I carried the glasses down to the table and set them out in neat rows, and then I went up to the house. There were big French doors leading into the living room, but I knew I shouldn't go in there. So I walked around to the side of the house until I saw a smaller door with a couple of garbage cans outside. I knocked. "It's open," somebody said, and I went in. It was a big kitchen with a modern gas stove and an electric icebox. The cook was working on a tray of canapés.

"I'm the bartender," I said. "I'm looking for the liquor."

"You're just a kid," she said.

I was getting tired of being told that. "I'm sixteen," I lied. "I look young for my age."

"Sixteen's a kid," she said. "Andy, the kid is here for the liquor." The chauffeur came out of somewhere and took me down to the cellar where the liquor was stored — four cases of it, as well as a lot of beer. I carried it down to the table a case at a time and set out two bottles each of gin, scotch, and bourbon. Then I found a washtub, put the beer on ice, and went back to the kitchen to fix up my lemon peels, orange slices, maraschino cherries, and so forth. "How many people are they having?" I said.

"Not many," the cook said. "About fifty. You going to be able to handle them alone?"

"Sure," I said. I carried my things down to the table and arranged them, and in a few minutes Mr. Waterman came down across the lawn. He was wearing white flannel trousers, a striped jacket, and a silk scarf around his neck. He looked like some movie actor.

"Got everything you need, Jack?"

"Yes, sir. Everything's okay."

The people began arriving at about four-thirty. Their cars filled up the driveway, and then they began to park them along the road. From where I was working I could see three Rolls-Royces, besides a few Caddies. Everybody was all dressed up. The women were wearing rustling silk dresses, and the men had on white suits or striped ones. Some of the older men were wearing straw hats. There were a few kids not much older than me there, and they were dressed up in white duck trousers and jackets, too. It was just like a party that you see in a movie. It gave me a thrill. I began to pretend that it was a movie and that some exciting thing was going to happen, like some guy would fall in love with somebody else's wife, or somebody would suddenly announce that there was a body in the bathtub and nobody could leave the premises. I knew that Sally would be crazy to see it herself. I figured that someday, if I got more jobs like it, I'd try to sneak her in. Maybe she could get some kind of a job as a waitress or something. There were a couple of maids walking around with trays of canapés. I figured Sally could learn to do that easy enough.

Mostly, though, I was too busy mixing drinks to

spend much time being in the movies. They certainly did a lot of drinking. By five-thirty they were getting sort of tight — talking loud and laughing a lot. I didn't have much trouble with the drinks. Most of them wanted plain scotch and soda. A few had Tom Collinses, and only a couple wanted martinis or whiskey sours. The only thing somebody wanted that I couldn't make was a brandy alexander. I knew that it was supposed to have crème de cacao in it, so I just said I didn't have the things for it and it was okay. Around six-thirty people began to drift away, but it was pretty gradual. There were still a lot of people there at seven, and the last ones didn't leave until after eight. The sun was going down over the lake, and the lawn was covered with cigarette butts, paper napkins, and pieces of canapé that had got dropped. Mr. Waterman and a woman who I figured was his wife stood there looking around. "What a mess," she said.

"I think it went well enough, though," he said.

"Oh sure, it was fine," she said.

He walked over to me. He seemed a little tight himself. "Any problems, Jack?"

"No, sir," I said. "Everything was okay."

"Well, you must have done a good job. I didn't hear any complaints, and this bunch will complain pretty quick if they don't like something."

"Do you want me to clean up the lawn?" I said.

"No, don't bother with that. The groundsman will do that in the morning. Put the rest of the liquor back in the cellar and wash up your glasses. Andy'll take you back to the boat club when you're ready to. Mrs. Waterman and I are going out for dinner." He reached into his jacket and took out his wallet. "Will five dollars do it?"

I had been expecting my usual twenty-five cents an hour, and I almost jumped. "Yes, sir," I said. "That's fine."

The Watermans left and I began carrying my stuff up to the kitchen. I put the liquor down in the cellar where I'd found it, and then I began washing up the glasses. The cook was putting some food away in the electric icebox. "You want anything to eat?" she said. "There's plenty of leftover canapés. I'm going to my room and have a nice sit-down and listen to Charlie McCarthy. Do you listen to him? He's a sketch. You never know what kind of trouble he's going to get into. And rude — the things he says to Bergen. They make me break out laughing."

"We don't have a radio," I said.

"Oh," she said. "That's too bad, there's a lot of good things on. Well, you can eat all the canapés you want, I'll just have to throw them out anyway, but don't touch anything else, hear? And when you're ready to go, tell Andy. He's in his room upstairs over the garage."

She left, and I went on washing the glasses and packing them back into the liquor boxes I had brought them in. In my mind I was thinking about what I would buy with five dollars. There were a lot of things I wanted. I needed a new mackinaw for winter, which would be seven or eight dollars, but I figured I'd have enough money at the end of the summer for that. The idea of getting a radio crossed my mind. I'd seen one in the Sears catalog for around ten dollars, but I was afraid it wouldn't be very good. I mean a regular big radio, like the one Charlie Franks' family had, would cost around thirty or forty dollars. Probably what I would get, I decided, was a pair of hi-cuts, which were boots that

115

came up to the middle of your calf and had a little jackknife pocket in the side. I'd always wanted a pair of hi-cuts. You could wear them in the summer to protect your feet if you were working on a farm or cutting wood or something, and in winter they were great because you didn't need galoshes or anything — just put on your hi-cuts and you'd be set for the day no matter how much snow there was. Gaines' clothing store had hi-cuts in their window for around three fifty.

Finally I got the glasses put away. I opened the electric refrigerator. There was a plate of canapés there, crackers or little circles of bread with stuff on them. The truth was, I didn't know what kind of food they were. Some of it looked like mashed up egg, and I knew that the little black beady stuff was caviar because I'd seen about it in a magazine once. But the rest of it was sort of mysterious pasty stuff with maybe an olive or something stuck in the top.

I was pretty much alone in the house, I realized. I figured that there was a maid around somewhere, but the cook was listening to the radio, the chauffeur was in the garage, and the Watermans were gone. I decided I would try to see what it felt like to be a millionaire. How would I do that? I decided to have a drink. I'd never really drunk much liquor, just sips of leftovers down at the club, which I'd snuck to see what they were like. I didn't like the taste of liquor much. The one I liked best was a whiskey sour. So I made myself a whiskey sour and then I got out the canapés and sat down at the kitchen table to eat and drink what the rich had been eating and drinking all afternoon.

I made myself sit up straight and try to eat real

politely the way rich people did. I took a few little sips of the cocktail, not gulping it or anything, and then I picked up one of the canapés—one which looked like it was made of egg and would be safe to start with. I had a few nibbles of it in a polite way. It wasn't bad, except for the anchovy on top, so I finished it off. Then I tried a caviar one. It was terrible, sort of salty and bitter tasting, but I finished it off, washing it down with some whiskey sour, because I wanted to be able to tell Sally that I'd eaten caviar. Then I began on some of the paste ones to see which types I could eat. I was pretty hungry. It was hard not to pick out all the egg ones and stuff them into my mouth.

Suddenly I realized that I wasn't feeling like a millionaire. A millionaire would like all this junk, and besides, he wouldn't be eating in the kitchen, he'd be eating in his own dining room. At the end of the room there wre swinging doors, which I figured went out into the dining room. I got up, pushed them open, and looked out. It was the dining room, all right. It had a huge fancy table in the middle, with twelve chairs around it. Against the wall was a great big sideboard with some silver on it — platters and pitchers and teapots — and hanging on the walls some kind of tapestries like from a museum. I stood there looking around and listening. There weren't any sounds of people, except the faint noise of the cook's radio. I went back into the kitchen, picked up my cocktail and the plate of canapés, pushed through the swinging doors and sat down at the head of the table.

I guess I wouldn't have done it if I hadn't drunk half a whiskey sour. I knew I would get into trouble if I was caught. I mean riffraff weren't supposed to go wandering around rich people's houses. The cook would give me hell, which would be bad enough, but if Mr. or Mrs. Waterman caught me, they'd throw me out and that would be the end of the bartending jobs for him. So it made me sort of nervous to be sitting there, but it made me feel sort of important, too. I tried to pretend that it was all mine, that I was the son of some rich man. And I sat there thinking to myself, well, will I go for a moonlight spin on the lake in my Gar Wood, or drive the Caddy up to Worcester for a movie, or call up a lot of girls and have Andy go around and get them? It was hard to decide. I figured a rich man must spend a lot of time trying to make up his mind about what he wanted to do.

Finally I finished off all the canapés that tasted good enough to eat. There was a little whiskey sour left, so I drank that up, too. Then I stood up. I felt a little dizzy from the drink. I took out my handkerchief and wiped up the crumbs and the wet spots from my glass, and then I started for the kitchen with the glass and the plate. At the swinging doors I stopped and looked around, trying to memorize it all so I could tell Sally about it. I went around the room from left to right, and when I got to the silverware I stopped. What was it worth, I wondered? Probably hundreds of dollars. Maybe even thousands of dollars. I knew from detective books I'd read that silver tea sets and stuff like that could be worth thousands of dollars if it was especially old or vaulable in some other way.

And what was to stop me from quickly packing it all into one of the empty liquor boxes and taking it home with me? The chauffeur wouldn't remember whether I'd brought in three boxes or four. There would be nothing to it. I went over to the sideboard to have a closer look. It was some kind of a set with the same curlicue pattern on the handles of the pitchers and around the edges of the bowls. There was a teapot, a sugar dish, a cream pitcher, a couple of other big pitchers, besides some vegetable dishes, a gravy boat, and some serving spoons and ladles. I saw right away that there was more than I could pack in one box: it'd take two or three boxes, and I figured that the chauffeur would notice if I had that many extra boxes. And what would I do with the stuff when I got it home? The Watermans would discover that it was missing the minute they got home. Maybe the cook or one of the maids would happen to come into the dining room and notice it sooner than that. Somebody might even notice while I was putting it in the station wagon. Of course they'd suspect me right away. If I was able to get away with it and get it hidden I'd be okay. I mean the cops would be sure to question me about it, but they couldn't prove anything if they couldn't catch me with the silverware. After all, there'd been a lot of other people wandering around the house that day — all the guests at the cocktail party.

But it was too risky. Suppose the cook came into the kitchen just as I was packing it up? Or suppose they got the cops on me before I could hide the stuff?

Then I had another thought. Why couldn't I steal just one thing — maybe a teapot — and then sort of push the things around it together so it didn't look like anything was missing? I could put the pot under

119

my shirt, whip into the kitchen, and quickly pack it under the glasses in one of the boxes. I began to feel pretty nervous. Would I do it? The best thing would be to take some of the glasses out of one of the boxes, so I could just drop the teapot in and close the box up in a couple of seconds. Besides, I was still holding the canapé plate and the whiskey sour glass. I pushed open the kitchen door.

The cook was coming through her door into the kitchen. "Where do you think you're going?" she said.

"I was looking for you," I said. "I thought this was your door."

"Well, it isn't," she said. "Just don't be wandering around this house."

"I didn't mean to," I said. "I just wanted to tell you I was going."

She believed me. I picked up a carton of glassware and began carrying it out to the station wagon. I had one lesson, anyway: if I was going to do any stealing, I'd better not do it on the spur of the moment, but plan it out carefully first.

7

I did a lot of thinking about whether I ought to tell Sally about it or not. On one side of it, I was afraid she might blab to Margene Sheckley or somebody, and then it would get around everywhere. On the other side, I figured if I was actually going to do any stealing, I'd have to tell her. I mean if I suddenly began showing up with a lot of money, she'd be suspicious about where it was coming from. Besides, I might need somebody to help me steal. I liked the idea of having her in on it with me. It makes things less scary to have somebody in on them with you.

It was pretty late when I got home — nine-thirty when we got to the boat club to drop off the glasses and then almost ten by the time the chauffeur drove me home. I wouldn't let him see where I lived; I made him drop me off up Main Street a ways, in front of another house. Then I walked home. Dad was out. The baby was in bed and Sally was sitting up in the kitchen in her pajamas reading *The Yearling,* which was a big best-seller she'd got from the library. I knew she was waiting up to hear about the rich people.

So I told her all about it — about how the house looked and mixing the drinks and the cook and the chauffeur and the Rolls-Royce.

"You rode with a chauffeur?" she said.

"He drove me home."

"Why didn't you have him honk the horn so I could look out the window?" she said.

"I'm not his boss, I couldn't make him honk the horn."

"Didn't you sit in the back and say, 'Home, James, and stuff?" she said.

"Naw, I sat up front with him. I'm a servant just like he is."

"Were the ladies wearing long dresses?"

"Not too long. They came down to their ankles. Well not that low, maybe. I sort of forget."

"Silk dresses?" she asked.

"I guess so," I said. "I'm not sure what silk looks like."

"What did they give you to eat?"

"I ate up the leftover canapés. Sal, I ate some caviar."

"Real caviar? What did it taste like?" she said.

"It was pretty salty."

"Salty?" she said. "I thought caviar was sweet. Why would it be so famous if it was salty?"

"I guess rich people have different kinds of mouths than us riffraff. A lot of the canapé junk was pretty gooky. Sour or bitter or salty."

"What else?"

"Well, the thing was, Sally, I made myself a cocktail and ate my supper in their dining room."

"Were you allowed to do that?" she said.

"Of course not," I said. "They don't want riffraff sitting around on their chairs. If they'd have known I did that, they'd have probably kicked me out."

"Were you scared?"

"Scared? What for?"

"In case they kicked you out," she said.

"No, I wasn't scared," I said. "Sally, it was the most fantastic room. Just like a movie. This big table with fancy chairs around it and these tapestries and on the sideboard a whole pile of silver teapots and stuff."

"Teapots?"

"A silver tea set and silver pitchers and big ladles. Things like that."

"God," she said.

"I figured it was worth a heck of a lot of money. Maybe even a thousand dollars."

"A thousand dollars?"

"Well, it's hard to know for sure. I mean you would have to take it to an expert to find out."

"I guess the Watermans would know," she said.

"Sal," I looked around just in case Henry was out of bed listening in, and lowered my voice to a whisper. "Sal, I was going to steal some of it."

"No," she said.

"Yes I was. I had it planned out in my mind that I'd quickly grab a teapot off the shelf, stick it under my shirt, race into the kitchen with it, and jam it down into one of the boxes I had the glasses in. Then I'd sort of shuffle the other things around so they wouldn't notice that it was missing right away."

123

"Jack, you wouldn't really do it."

"I almost did it, too, but the cook happened to come out of her room just at that minute."

"You could get into a lot of trouble," she said.

"Not if you don't get caught."

"You really wouldn't have."

"Yes, I would have," I said. "I was going to." But the truth was, I didn't know if I would have or not. I'd never know for sure until I tried it.

On Wednesday Dad went down to New York. He took the eight A.M. train just in case he might find a gig for the evening. Sally made him a couple of bologna sandwiches to take with him. "I'll be home sometime Friday," he said, "unless I have a gig."

"Dad," Sally said, "do you think you'll have the money for my outfit?"

"I feel lucky today," he said. "I have the feeling that things are about to turn around."

"Do you really think you'll get the money?"

"Sal," he said, "I'll steal it if I have to." Then he walked out the door with his trombone and his suitcase.

I waited until the door was shut. "Sally, I wish you wouldn't keep getting your hopes up."

"He promised."

"Well I know," I said. "But suppose he doesn't get any gigs? Suppose he has bad luck?"

"He promised," she said.

Suddenly it came to me that it didn't have anything to do with bad luck. The truth was that if Dad really cared about Sally having her new outfit he'd figure out a way to get it for her. I mean eight bucks was a lot of dough, but it wasn't *that* much. Dad probably spent two or three bucks a week for cigarettes and beers down at the Colonial. Then he was always buying some record, which usually cost fifty cents. It just seemed to me that he could figure out a way to get the eight bucks if he wanted to. It made me scared to think that maybe he wouldn't get Sal her outfit. I just hoped that he would. Still, I knew she'd better not get her hopes up.

"He's always promising stuff," I said.

"But this time he really promised."

"Sometimes he doesn't keep his promises," I said.

She stamped her foot. "Don't say that, Jack. It isn't true."

I could see that she was getting mad. "Well, it is true, Sal."

"No, no," she shouted. "Don't say that anymore."

I knew I should drop it, but I was mad myself. Why should he get the credit for keeping promises when he didn't? "It's true, Sal."

She jumped out at me and hit me on the chest. "Stop saying that," she shrieked.

I grabbed her hands so she couldn't hit me. "Damn it, don't do that, Sally, or I'll slug you."

"Don't say that anymore."

She struggled to get her hands loose, and I knew she was going to try to kick me. "Let me go," she said.

"If you stop hitting me."

She kicked, but I was ready for it and jumped my feet aside. "Cut it out, or I'll really slam you," I said.

"Let me go!" she shouted.

"All right," I said. I let her go. We stood there panting and staring at each other.

"Don't say that anymore," she said. I didn't say

anything and she stalked off to her room, with her nose poking up in the air and her behind switching back and forth like the tail of a cat.

On Friday, Dad called to say that he wouldn't be home until Saturday or Sunday. He hadn't got a gig yet, but he had a possibility of one for Saturday night; he'd have to wait and see. On Saturday afternoon he called again and talked to Sally — of course I was at work. The Saturday gig had fallen through, but there was a wedding on Sunday afternoon that seemed pretty definite, so he'd be home Monday. He called again on Sunday. I talked with Sally about it Sunday night when I got home from work. She was all excited. "He got two gigs," she said. "He got one Saturday after all, besides the wedding gig on Sunday. He says there's plenty of work down in New York. We're turning the corner, he says."

"He always says that," I said.

"This time is different," she said.

I didn't want to have any more fights over it. "I hope so," I said. "Did you ask him about your new outfit?"

"No," she said.

"You better bring it up as soon as he gets home. Make him take you down to Gaines' right away while he's in a good mood."

Dad got home around supper time on Monday. Sally was cooking and Henry was setting the table. Henry leaped up on him and Sally gave him a big hug. I hung back; I didn't feel like getting in on the hugging. But Dad didn't even notice. He threw his arm around my shoulder and gave me a squeeze. Then he opened his suitcase and began flinging his clothes around, looking for things. He'd brought

126

back a fancy fountain pen for Sally and a fake watch for Henry and an official baseball for me, which was kind of the wrong present because of what it reminded me of. He also had a stack of records for himself. "Lots of work down there," he said. He gave us a wink. "As long as the union doesn't find out." It was just like him to spend all that money for presents when we were almost broke, but I could see that he figured he could always whip down to New York and get more gigs. Anyway, it cheered us all up to have him back.

So we sat down to dinner, which was meat loaf, something else Sally was practicing on because somebody had told her that you couldn't ruin meat loaf. It was pretty good, actually, a little pink inside, but that didn't bother us. Then Dad told us about New York. "There's plenty of work for a good professional musician. The thing I have to do is work out my union card."

"What's that?" Sally said.

"To join Local 802 down there I have to be a resident of New York for six months. There's a friend of mine in the city, a trombone player I used to work with in the Mal Hallett Orchestra, and I'm using his place as an address. He'll say I've been living there and in six months I can get my union card."

"But you're not really living there," Sally said.

"I know. It doesn't matter. Everybody does it. You just have to have some proof that you've been living in New York for six months."

"Are we going to live there?" Henry said.

"Maybe," he said. "We'll see how it goes. I plan to go down a lot from now on. There's a lot of work

127

outside the city, in the suburbs, like Westchester County or out on Long Island. They've got the bucks in those fancy suburbs, lots of country clubs and golf clubs. Dances every Saturday night, and when they lay out one of those socialite weddings, they don't care what they spend on the band; they'll bring in a fifteen-piece orchestra if they want. With all that work there's a lot of last-minute scrambling around for substitutes. Work's bound to fall in if you're down there."

"If we move to New York can I get a two-wheeler?" Henry said.

Dad patted him on the head. "Sure," he said. "Maybe we'll get an apartment by Central Park, it's a terrific place for bikes; you can ride for miles there."

"Dad —" Sally said, and I knew she was going to bring up the outfit.

"Who knows," Dad said, "by this time next year maybe the depression will be over and we'll be rolling in money again. The way the swing boom is going, I might have a band of my own. The Warren Lundquist Orchestra playing for your dining and dancing pleasure from Frank Daley's Meadowbrook." He speared into his meatloaf. "Very good, Sal." He swallowed quickly so he could go on talking. "I wouldn't want to get into all this heavy swing like Barnet or Basie. My idea would be an easier swing with a nice danceable beat. More like the Casa Loma bunch. That's what people like. You give them a good danceable beat and you'll have them eating out of the palm of your hand." He began to cut off another piece of meat loaf.

"Dad," Sally sort of blurted out, "can we get my outfit tomorrow?"

His hands stopped cutting and he looked straight ahead. "Your outfit?"

"My new outfit?"

"I haven't forgotten about it," he said.

"Can we get it tomorrow?"

He looked down at his plate and pushed a piece of meat loaf around with his fork. "When are you supposed to have it by?"

"Thursday," she said.

"Oh," he said. "Well, I'd rather not do it tomorrow. I've got a lot of things to catch up on. There's still plenty of time. We'll do it later in the week." He leaned back. "Now, tell me how you kids got along while I was gone." And of course then we all knew that he'd spent everything he made down in New York.

I looked at him; he didn't seem worried or upset, he just wanted to change the subject and get out of it. I wanted to leave the table. "I don't feel too good," I said. "I'm going to go lie down."

"What's the matter, Jack?" he said.

"I just don't feel too good. I'll be all right in a minute." I got up and went into Sally's room and lay down on her bed. There wasn't any way out of it anymore: my father wasn't any better than a bum. I'd been kidding myself. I guess I'd been kidding myself for years, trying to think that he was a good father, that he was just having bad luck. But I couldn't kid myself anymore. He wasn't a good father, he was neglectful and he messed things up. Here we were living in this dumpy place, and eating franks and beans half the time, and not even having enough milk sometimes. And he kept saying it was bad luck, it was hard times, it was the depression; but I noticed that Dave Johnson's family didn't live on franks and beans, and Charlie Franks had his own room and a radio. Oh Dad was jolly and cheerful and always looking on the bright side; but what was the use of that when you were living on franks and beans all the time? And it came to me that I'd been looking on the bright side, too — I'd been looking on the bright side about Dad. I wasn't going to do that anymore.

Still, I didn't want to have to give Sally the money for her outfit. I only had saved up about twelve dollars. This was my fifth weekend at the boat club coming up. I'd made, counting tips and everything, thirty-one dollars and fifty cents. I kept it all written down on a piece of paper. But I'd spent most of it. Some of it I spent on junk like comic books, ice cream, and Mounds bars, which were my favorite. I tried to budget my junk down to fifty cents a week, which allowed for one five-cent ice-cream cone or candy bar after school every day, two comic books, and fifteen cents left over for the weekend. Then there was my school milk money, which was five cents a day, and two dollars I'd spent for four school trips to Boston — we went to the Arnold Arborteum and the Peabody Museum and some other places. And I'd bought some new socks, too. So out out of my thirty-one dollars I'd spent about only eight or nine on myself. But the trouble was that half the time Henry or Sally wouldn't have any milk money, and they'd ask me for it. Or we'd need bread or peanut butter and Dad wouldn't be around, so I'd go out and get it myself. Or Henry would need a quarter for a school project or Sally would need some money for the Girl Scouts. So in the end, all I had left was twelve dollars, and five of that was from tending bar at Mr. Waterman's house. I sure didn't want to spend any of it on Sal's outfit. I had plans for that money — hi-cuts and a mackinaw for the fall; and besides, if I could get days off this summer, I wanted to go up to Boston with Charlie for a few ball games.

But I couldn't stand for Sal not to have her outfit. She'd got her heart set on it. I knew how she felt. All the other kids would have new things for the school play, and there she'd be in one of her old dresses that was too short anyway. Oh, sure, a lot of families in Stevenstown weren't much better off than we were. Some of the mothers would have to sew dresses for their girls to be in the play or maybe even cut one of their sister's down. But Sally didn't have anyone to sew for her; and maybe even that would have been all right, but the truth was that Dad could have saved up the eight dollars or whatever it would be himself. He could have taken a day job just for a couple of days and made it that way. He could have got Sally her outfit he'd wanted to. Oh, I hated him for putting me on the spot. But there wasn't anything I could do about it; I couldn't stand for Sal not to have her outfit. So on Tuesday I brought it up with Sally.

Dad was out somewhere and Henry was in the backyard with some kid bouncing his ball on the cement. Sally was in her room lying on her bed reading a horse book.

"Did you finish *The Yearling* already?" I said.

"It was short," she said.

"Listen," I said, "did he say anything about your outfit?"

She went on reading her book.

"Did he?"

She didn't look up. "I don't want to talk about it," she said.

"Listen, Sal," I said, "I have enough money,"

She went on reading. "I don't want a new outfit anymore."

I didn't say anything for a minute. She was making it sort of hard for me to give her the money. "Yes, you do," I said finally.

"No, I don't." She put the book down. "Stop bothering me, I don't want to talk about it."

"Listen, I could give you the money and then Dad could pay me back when he gets some money."

"No," she said. "No, no." She put her hands over her ears. "If you don't go away I'm going to scream." She began to kick her feet on the bed.

I didn't know what to do. She was pretty upset.

"Listen, Sal —"

"Go away, go away," she shouted, with her hands still over her ears.

"Sal, I'm —"

She let out a big scream, "EEEEyaaaahh."

"All right, all right," I said. I left and went out to the bureau in the living room where I kept my clothes. My money was in a tin cigarette box, the flat fifty kind that Pall Malls came in. I took out eight dollars, closed up the box, and shut the drawer. Then I walked back into Sally's room. "Here," I said. I held out the money.

She didn't look up, she didn't say anything, but held the book up in front of her so I couldn't see her face.

"Here's eight dollars."

She didn't move or say anything at all. I put the

money down on the bed. "I'm putting the money here," I said.

She didn't answer.

"The money's here on the bed." I started to leave; and then she flung the book down, flipped over on her stomach, and began to cry as hard as she could. It was pretty embarrassing. I walked out of the room and shut the door.

Sally went down to Gaines' clothing store on Wednesday afternoon with Margene Sheckley and got her outfit. She left early Thursday morning wearing it, because she didn't want Dad to see it; and she took it off right after she came home from school. The funny thing was, when she wore it a couple of days later in front of him, he didn't even notice that it was new.

So the days went along. Dad had a good gig in Worcester and a couple of little ones. He kept talking about going down to New York again, but he didn't say when he would do it. It seemed to me that he was drifting, just sort of waiting for something to happen. He didn't seem to be planning anything. And I kept getting the feeling that we were drifting right into some big problem, which would end with the family being split up. I used to think about that a lot. I'd go over the money in my head, adding up how much money Dad was making and how much we were spending for rent and things, and it always came out with us in the hole. I wasn't sure exactly how much things cost, of course. I knew that the rent was twenty-five dollars a month, but I didn't know how much the gas bill was, or the electricity. I didn't know how much we owed at the grocery store, although I knew we owed something; we always had a bill there. And I didn't know what other bills we owed. But as close as I could figure, it just seemed to me that we weren't making enough money to get by. I knew how Dad figured; he wouldn't notice that; he'd just keep thinking, well, next week I'll get a few big gigs and pay it all off. But I didn't believe stuff like that anymore. And it just seemed to me that sooner or later we were going to go totally broke; and then the family would have to split up — Sally down in New Orleans with Grandpa and Grandma, poor Henry out in Chicago with Uncle Edgar and Aunt Mabel, and me, I didn't know where.

And it was just as clear as could be, that if the family was going to stay together, us kids would have to do it ourselves. Especially Sally and me. Mainly me. There wasn't any way around that. Dad just wasn't going to get us out of the mess. He was just going to drift along looking on the bright side, and one fine day we'd all be getting on trains to go different places.

If I could get the summer job at the boat club it would be a help. I could work seven days a week, maybe a total of seventy hours or so, which would amount to around twenty dollars a week, with tips. So far Mr. Slater hadn't said anything about it, but a couple of times he'd asked me when school would be out, and I figured it was in his mind. I resolved that if he didn't say anything about it soon, I'd bring it up myself. I'd have to. If he wasn't going to hire me for the summer, I'd have to start looking someplace else.

In the meantime Charlie Franks and I had begun working out together in a vacant lot past his house after school. At first we didn't want to have anything to do with baseball, it was too sickening to think about. But then we decided that we'd better go to the ball games, it would help us out with the coach the next year if he saw that we were interested in the team and were probably sorry for what we'd done. So we went to all the games, even the away games, when we could. I guess we were hoping he'd relent and let us back on the team. He noticed us all right; after a few games he'd sort of nod when he saw us there. But he didn't say anything about coming back on the team. The worst part of it was, I knew that I'd had a good chance of making it. The substitute fielders could field okay, but they couldn't hit worth beans. I figured I could have hit a little, even if I was having trouble with curves. So anyway, on days when the team didn't have a game, Charlie and I got in the habit of working out in his vacant lot, slamming grounders at each other to improve our fielding, working on our hook slides, and pitching batting practice to each other so we could work on our bunting.

One night when I came home around six o'clock from Charlie's there was a man standing at the back door talking to Sally. She was saying, "My father isn't home. He went out." I figured he was at the Colonial.

"When will he be back?" the man asked.

"I don't know," she said.

"I walked up. "What's going on?"

"He wants to see Dad. He say's we're behind on the rent."

The man turned around to look at me. He wasn't our regular landlord. I figured he was some kind of bill collector. "Behind on the rent?" I said. "How much?"

"Four months," he said.

That was a hundred dollars. I didn't know where we could get that.

"And there'll be another payment due at the end of May, too."

"I don't know when Dad will be home," I said. "I'll tell him."

"He'll be home for supper, won't he?"

"Sometimes he doesn't come home until late," Sally said. "He might be playing a gig."

The man looked suspicous. "He's a musician?"

"Yes," I said.

"I might have known," he said. "You'll be out of here soon enough. You tell him we're going to serve an eviction notice if we don't get something on this by Friday." Then he left.

I looked at Sally and she looked back. "I didn't know he wasn't paying the rent," I said.

"It's scary," she said. "I didn't think we owed that much money. I wonder if he owes other people, too."

"I figured all along we owed money," I said. "I didn't realize it would be that much. The thing is, if he's behind on the rent, he's probably behind on other bills, too. We might owe two hundred dollars."

"Two hundred dollars?" She looked pretty worried. "We could never get that."

"We'll have to talk to him," I said.

We went into the house. I was scared. I didn't want to have to treat my own father like a kid. I mean he was supposed to be the father. Why was I supposed to bawl him out about not paying the rent. "Have we got anything good to drink?" I said.

"There's some coffee in the pot," she said. "I could make some iced coffee."

I could tell she was feeling sorry for me, because she knew it was up to me to bring it up with Dad about the rent, being the oldest. "Sure," I said. "I'm thirsty."

She poured the coffee in a glass, chipped some ice off the block in the icebox, and put it in. "Do you want some milk?"

"Sure," I said. She put in milk and sugar and gave me the glass. I didn't drink coffee much, but I liked iced coffee if there was plenty of milk and sugar in it. And I was sitting there drinking it with Sally when Dad came in.

"Hi, kids," he said.

"Hi," we both said.

He was carrying a new record. He walked through the kitchen and out into the living room. I knew I ought to say something, but I didn't.

"Are you going to ask him?" Sally said.

"In a minute," I said.

We could hear Dad fooling around with the victrola. In a moment the music began. It was some swing band, but I couldn't tell which. We sat there listening to it until the record was finished. Then Dad came back into the kitchen. "How did you like that?" he said. "It's the Casa Loma Orchestra. That's the kind of sound I want for my band. Nice danceable tempo, not too jazzy, but with a good swing. Not too many solos, lots of smooth ensemble. I'd like to use unison trombones a lot."

"Dad," I said.

"It would be a good gimmick for me. Feature the trombone section on a lot of numbers."

"Dad," I said. "There was a man here about the rent."

"The rent?" he said. "Oh?"

"He said we owed for four months."

He scratched his head. "Four months? That can't be right. I'm sure it isn't that much."

"That's what he said."

"That's right, Dad," Sally said. "He said four months."

"I didn't think it was that much."

Nobody said anything.

"Well," he said, "I guess I'll have to do something about it."

Sally and I didn't say anything.

"I'll give him something on account."

"He said if we didn't pay up by Friday he would evict us," I said.

"Oh, I don't think they'd do that," Dad said.

"He said he would."

"I'll give him something on account. Don't worry about it."

"Dad, what'll we do if he evicts us?"

"Don't worry about it, Jack. I'll take care of it. Listen everybody, what about going to the movies tonight? It's *Test Pilot* with Clark Gable and Spencer Tracy."

"But what'll we do?"

"Jack, stop looking on the gloomy side all the time," he said. "I'll take care of it tomorrow. Tonight we're going to have a nice supper and then we're all going to the movies."

I got up my courage. "Dad, how much other stuff do we owe?"

He looked at me. "That's my business, it isn't your business. I'll worry about it."

"We'll have to worry about it, too, if we're

evicted," I said. I knew he was getting mad, but I was getting pretty tired of him dodging around the subject.

"Damn it, Jack, I told you to forget about it. I'm the father around here, I'll do the worrying. Now you two forget about it. I'll take care of it."

I stood up. "Dad, we have a right to know about it. It affects us, too."

"God damn it, Jack, don't give me any nonsense about your rights." He was pretty near shouting. "You're just a kid, this is my business."

"I agree with Jack," Sally said.

"You shut up, Sally," he said.

I was scared, but I was sore, too. "Dad, how come you go out and buy a record when we owe all this money for rent?"

"God damn it, Jack, I won't have this." He was really shouting now. I'd never seen him that mad before. "I don't want to hear another word about this. You're not going to start telling me what to do with my money, and that's final."

"Damn it, Dad," I shouted, "we have a right in it too. Some of it's my money, too. I had to buy Sally her new outfit."

The minute I said that I knew I shouldn't have. He reached back his hand and then he smacked me as hard as he could across my face. My head snapped back and suddenly I was sitting on the floor. My head was swinging around and around and the whole side of my face stung. "You son of a bitch," I shouted. Tears were rolling down my face. I jumped up and ran out of the door crying and cursing as I went.

8

The trouble with running away from home is that sooner or later you have to go back again. I walked around crying and mad for a while trying to think of what to do. I figured I could go to the Frankses' house and spend the night, but I didn't want to explain what had happened to anybody, not even Charlie. I didn't want anybody to know that we were going to be evicted. But I had to sleep someplace. So I finally decided to go out to the boat club. There were a lot of deck chairs on the clubhouse porch. I could easily take the cushions off them and spread them around on the floor and sleep there. So I began walking out to the lake. Most of the way I was raging at Dad. First I had an idea of getting a baseball bat out of my closet, catching him from behind, and smashing him on the head with it. Gritting my teeth, I could almost feel in my hands how it would feel to smash a bat over his head. Next I had a calmer idea of catching him when he was asleep, tying him down to the bed, and torturing him with a whip or something. Finally, when I had walked a couple of miles, I calmed down to where I was just thinking about going to the police or whoever you would go to and getting him arrested for not paying his bills.

It was a nice night for walking. The peepers were going a mile a minute, and I could smell all sorts of sweet things in the air: new-cut grass when I was going by one house, lilacs at another place, apple blossoms at another. It was warm, too — just the kind of spring night that tells you that summer is just around the corner. I wished I could have enjoyed it, but I was too sore to. So I just kept on walking and after a while I got to the boat club. I climbed over the big iron gate — I was getting used to doing that — and walked up the gravel to the clubhouse. This time I wasn't worried about anyone seeing me. If a cop came along I'd just tell him the truth — that I worked here, and I had a fight with my father and came out looking for a place to sleep.

I came around the clubhouse and up onto the porch. The lake was just beautiful. The air was a little misty, but the moon was shining through it anyway and splashing light all over the lake and the docks and the boats tied up to it. The night was still. The lake was dead calm and the boats at the dock sat there silent and unmoving, their masts sticking up like ghosts. I stood there for a minute looking at it. It was all so beautiful I couldn't stand not doing something. So I took off all my clothes and walked down to the end of the dock between the rows of ghost masts. At the end of the dock I stopped. Being

141

riffraff, I'd never been allowed to swim at the boat club. I didn't know how deep it was off the end of the dock. In the dark the lake was just a black patch with the sheet of moonlight coming across it. But I'd seen people dive off the end of the dock, so I took a deep breath and dove. The water was cold and it shocked me. I swam out a few strokes and then I turned around and sat there treading water. The moonlight shone on the dock and the boats and the clubhouse. The Pines made a tall, jagged black wall behind the clubhouse. It looked so rich, and right then it was all mine. There was nobody around. I could do anything I wanted. After a couple of minutes I began to shiver. Slowly I swam back to the dock and heaved myself up out of the water. I sat there at the end of the dock. After the coldness of the water the air felt warm. In a minute I got up, went over to the nearest boat, and climbed into it, just to see how it felt to be in a boat. The seat was covered with dew, but that didn't bother me because I was still wet. I sat there slowly drying out. Finally I was dry enough and I went back to the clubhouse, put my clothes back on, and began taking cushions off the chairs and spreading them around on the porch floor. Then I lay down on them.

In about two minutes I realized that it wasn't so warm out as I'd thought. Walking along it had seemed warm enough, but lying still was different. I pulled my legs up tight to try to keep warmer, but it didn't help any. I sat up. There were a lot of things in the clubhouse I could use for blankets — tarpaulins, and a couple of sou'westers Mr. Slater kept in his office, and plenty of beach towels.

And a sleeping bag.

The minute I thought of that I went cold and my heart began to race. I didn't know how much money was in it — it might only be forty or fifty dollars. But it might be a lot more than that, too. Suppose it was a hundred? It would be enough to pay the rent so at least we wouldn't be evicted. And maybe Dad would change. Maybe now that we'd had a fight and he saw how terrible we all felt, he might decide to get a day job. Maybe he would feel terrible about hitting me and take a day job just to apologize. If only we didn't get evicted.

But suppose it was only thirty dollars? Suppose Mr. Slater had only just begun to use the sleeping bag for a hiding place? There might be only five or ten dollars in it. It wouldn't be worth taking the risk for that little money. But I didn't think that. That big brown envelope had already been in the sleeping bag, so he must have put money in it before. I took a deep breath. I was scared all right; but I knew I was going to do it. I knew I would at least open up the sleeping bag and find out how much was in it.

But could I get in? Mr. Slater had surely locked the place up tight. I got up and tried the front door, the one that went into the clubhouse from the porch. It was locked. I went around to the back door next to the storeroom. It was locked, too. I knew that I could slide through the storeroom window if I was willing to break the glass again, but I didn't want to go through that again.

The only other possibility was the big windows that ran along the porch side of the clubhouse. I went back to the porch and began checking the windows. They were all locked. I wasn't surprised. Mr.

Slater was pretty careful about locking things up, especially since the robbery. In the dark I tried to get a look at the catch on one of the windows. There was just about enough moonlight to make it out. It was one of those ordinary window locks that you swivel to lock. I knew that sometimes you could open that kind of lock with your jackknife. You slipped the blade up between the upper and lower frames and pushed it against the part of the lock that swiveled. If it wasn't too tight you could push it back.

I got out my jackknife and went along the windows checking the locks to see if there was one that wasn't closed all the way. I didn't see any, though; Mr. Slater was really careful. So I picked out a window and worked my blade up into the crack between the frames. When I got it most of the way up I began to push it against the swivel. It slid open just like that, as easy as pie. I guess Mr. Slater was careful to keep them oiled. I put my jackknife down on the window sill. Then I pushed the window up, climbed through, and closed it down again. Of course I wouldn't be able to lock it up when I left, but I figured Mr. Slater wouldn't think anything of it if one window happened to be unlocked. He would think he left it open by mistake.

It was pretty dark inside there. I didn't want to turn on a light. There were a lot of houses across the lake that faced the clubhouse, and they'd be sure to notice if the clubhouse lights suddenly went on. Of course they might not think anything of it; but with the robbery so recent in people's minds, there was a good chance somebody would call the cops if they saw anything suspicious. It would be one thing for a cop to find me asleep on the porch; but they'd sure make trouble if they discovered I'd broken in.

There was a big flashlight in Mr. Slater's office on the shelf where he kept the medicine cabinet. I sort of felt my way across the clubhouse, bumping into chairs here and there, until I got to the office. The door was open. I fumbled my way past Mr. Slater's desk, found the flashlight on the shelf, and switched it on, keeping it carefully pointed downwards so the light wouldn't show out the window. Even pointed downwards, it threw enough shadowy light around the room so I could make out what was on the shelves above. Just about, anyway. The shelves went all the way up to the ceiling. There was all sorts of junk on them — boat fittings, and paint, and various flags and pennants that the club flew from time to time, and flares, and tools. But I didn't see the sleeping bag. Maybe Mr. Slater had taken it home. I was disappointed, but kind of relieved, too. Still, I wasn't ready to give up. Cautiously I raised the flashlight up a little to throw more light on the upper shelves. And then I saw it. The reason why I hadn't spotted it before was because it was right in the corner. There was a big box of something next to it, and Mr. Slater had propped a life ring up in front of it, so you'd be less likely to notice it.

I lay the flashlight down on the floor so that it would shine just enough light upwards for me to see what I was doing, pulled the chair out from behind Mr. Slater's desk, and stood on it. It was one of those swivel chairs that go round and round, and sort of tippy. I knew I shouldn't move too fast, but I didn't want to dawdle around, either. I lifted the life ring off where it was leaning up against the sleeping bag, then pulled the sleeping bag down and flung it onto the floor and put the life ring back. Moving carefully, I jumped down from the chair, picked up the sleeping bag, and switched off the light.

My heart was going a mile a minute and I was nervous as a cat. I just wanted to get out of there; if anybody had seen the light moving around in the clubhouse they could have the police here any minute. I went over to the sill. I figured I'd better take the sleeping bag outside and open it up there in the safety of the pines behind the parking lot. I bumped my way across the club room as fast as I could and climbed through the window. As I slid over the sill I heard a clunk; I realized I'd left my jackknife sitting there and had knocked it off onto the porch floor. But I was in too much of a hurry to pick it up; I'd get it later. I raced along the porch, around the clubhouse, and into the pines that bordered the parking lot. Then I flung the sleeping bag down, dropped down beside it, and lay flat, listening.

With the night so still there was no sound except my heart pounding away. I raised up my head and cocked my ears around, half expecting to hear a siren or the sound of car wheels crunching down the driveway. But there wasn't anything. So I raised myself up on my knees. If anyone came, I could go flat, and they wouldn't see me unless they came into the pines with a flashlight, looking for me. Then I unrolled the sleeping bag and reached down inside. The envelope was still there. I pulled it out and held it up into the patchy moonlight filtering down through the pines. The bag was sort of wrinkled and dirty. I bent the clasp at the top back, opened it up — and suddenly my heart began to thump. The

146

envelope was loaded with money — fives and tens and even some twenties. I pulled it all out and dumped it on the sleeping bag. My hands were shaking, and I was too nervous to count it properly, but it was over three hundred dollars.

I figured some of it must be kickback money, but there was too much of it to be just that. He must have been stealing out of the boat club bank account. Of course there was no way I could know for sure how he did it. Once in a while the members' committee went over the books to check up, but since Mr. Slater kept the accounts himself he probably just changed the numbers around to cover up what he was stealing — put down some phony expenses or something. Anyway, however he did it, I was sure it was crooked money. Nobody hides three hundred dollars in a sleeping bag way up in the corner of a shelf if it isn't crooked money. And it seemed to me that if he'd already stolen that much money this early in the season, he probably was making himself an extra thousand dollars a year in crooked money.

The question was, would I steal it? I figured I could get away with it. Mr. Slater couldn't report it to the cops. The minute it got out that he'd been hiding money in a sleeping bag, the members' committee would get suspicious and start checking up on him. One thing was sure: if I took the money, Mr. Slater couldn't make a fuss over it.

For a second thing, how would he know it was me because I was around there a lot, but so were a lot of other people. I mean there were groundskeepers in and out, and delivery people, and lots of kids, and of course the members. There would be no reason for him to suspect me over anybody else. Well, some reason. I guess I would be the most logical person to suspect because I was around the clubhouse more than anybody else except him. But still, what was he going to do, come up to me and say, "Jack, did you steal the money out of my sleeping bag?" I was the honest kid who'd returned a wallet with over a hundred and fifty dollars in it. No, once he discovered it was missing he'd just have to keep quiet about it and suffer. Oh, he'd be sure to check around to see if anybody was suddenly spending a lot of money — buying a lot of new clothes or a new car or something. But I wouldn't be that stupid. I'd be using the money to pay rent and the back bills, and he wouldn't know anything about that.

Then there was another thing: how long would it take him to discover that the money was missing? I didn't think he would open up the sleeping bag to put money in it every day. Probably he would do it only when he had piled up a bit of crooked money — maybe once a week or something like that. So that made it even safer: he might not know about it for a week. All I had to do was stick the money in my pocket, roll up the sleeping bag, and put it back exactly as I'd found it. It was as safe as could be.

But would I do it? The money was lying there on the sleeping bag, with a little bit of the moonlight coming down on it. I tried to calm myself down a little; and when I got a little quieter I picked up the money and counted it carefully, trying to pretend that it was just Monopoly money. It came out to three hundred and fifty dollars.

I had the kind of feeling you get when you're about to jump off something high — a rock over the lake or off somebody's porch roof on a dare. First you lean forward, and just then you get a swooshy feeling and you lean back again. You do that a few times, and then all at once you jump, and there's no knowing why you jumped that time when you hadn't jumped all the other times. It was the same with the money. I stood there thinking about shoving the money into my back pocket; my hand would jerk of its own accord, but it wouldn't go into my back pocket, and I'd be still standing there with the money in my hand. Three times it jerked like that, and three times I was still standing there with the money in my hand, and then all of a sudden I shoved the money in my back pocket, and it was done.

Now I was in a hurry. Quickly I swooped up some pine needles and shoved them into the envelope to fatten it up. I closed the clasp, slid the envelope down into the sleeping bag, rolled up the bag, and tied it up. I wished I remembered exactly how it had been rolled and tied, but I figured Mr. Slater wouldn't notice anything until he got the bag down to unroll it himself.

With the sleeping bag under my arm I slipped to the edge of the pine trees and looked around. I was kind of startled to see that everything was the same as it had been — the moonlight shone on the lake, the boats stood ghostly at the dock. So much had happened inside of me, it seemed like the world ought to be different. But it wasn't. I ran out of the cover of the pines, across the parking lot, and around to the front of the clubhouse. I flung the bag through the window, climbed through after it, fumbled my way into Mr. Slater's office and found the flashlight again. Shielding it carefully, I climbed

149

up onto the chair and put the sleeping bag back where it had been. It took me a minute to get the life ring to stand up in front of it. I wanted to make sure it was up there nice and solid and wouldn't come tumbling off when somebody slammed a door. But in a minute I got it. Then I put the flashlight and the chair away, went out the window, and shut it. Mr. Slater would probably notice that it was unlocked when he went around opening the place up in the morning, but he wouldn't think anything about it. There was no way I could lock it, anyway — you could only swivel the catch one way with a jack-knife. So I raced down the driveway, climbed over the big iron gate, and began jogging back into town.

I was excited by having so much money, but pretty scared, too. That lump in my back pocket felt as big as a loaf of bread. It seemed to me that if anyone saw me the first thing they'd notice would be that I had a huge lump in my pocket. I knew that was silly, but still, I wanted to get home as fast as possible to get the money off me. I wasn't sure of where I'd hide it, but there were plenty of places. Nobody would think of looking around our old place for money.

Sally was sitting at the kitchen table reading a horse book when I got home. "Where's Dad?" I said.

"Out," she said. "Where did you go?"

"I'll tell you," I said.

"Your eye is swollen."

"Is it?" I said. I went into the bathroom and looked in the mirror. It was puffed up a little, but not too bad. I ran some cold water over a washcloth and held it up against my eye for a couple of minutes; but I was too impatient to get rid of the money, and I quit and went back into the kitchen.

"Does it hurt?" Sally said.

"No," I said. "I didn't even know it was swollen. It hurt when he hit me, but it doesn't anymore." I sat down in the rocker. "When did Dad go out?"

"Right after you ran out. He was pretty upset. He kept saying, 'Sally, I shouldn't have hit him, but he was pushing me too hard.'"

"It's his own damn fault," I said.

"You shouldn't have told him you paid for my outfit. It hurt his feelings."

"I know it did," I said. "But that isn't my fault." Then I stood up. "Is the baby asleep?"

"Yes," she said.

"I'm going to check," I said. I went out, slipped open the bedroom door a crack, and peeked in. The light from the door fell across Henry's face. His eyes were closed and he was breathing slow. I shut the door. Then I went back into the kitchen, reached into my back pocket, took out the lump, and waved it in front of Sally. "Look, Sally," I whispered. "Look."

"Jack," she said. "Where did you get it?"

"I'll tell you," I said. "Guess how much it is?"

"Twenty dollars?"

"More," I said.

"Fifty?"

"More, more," I said. I was sort of dancing around in front of her, waving the money.

"More?" she said. "A hundred?"

"More," I said. "Way more."

"I don't believe it. How much?"

"Guess."

"Two hundred?"

"More, more."

"I don't believe it."

151

I couldn't stand the suspense anymore. "Three hundred and fifty dollars, Sally."

"Three hundred and fifty dollars? My God, Jack, where did you get it?"

"I stole it," I whispered. "From Mr. Slater."

"Jack, Jack." She jumped up, and began sort of dancing around, too.

"I did. I stole it." Suddenly I realized that Dad might come in at any time. "We've got to find a place to hide it, Sal."

"Let me see it," she said. "Please, Jack, let me feel it."

"I handed it to her. "Come on," I said, "help me think of a place."

She flipped it with her hand. "How did you get it?"

"I'll tell you in a minute. Help me find a place before Dad comes."

"We could hide it in my bureau," she said. "Dad never fools around in there."

"We'll wake up the baby."

"Well, where then?"

Hiding it in her bureau was a good idea. Dad never bothered about Sally's clothes — Sally washed and ironed them herself. She kept all her things neat. She was always rearranging her things; she never let anybody mess around with her stuff. "Okay," I said. "We'll hide it in your bureau tomorrow. But we have to find someplace to put it tonight."

We decided, finally, to put it in the broom closet in the kitchen. It was just a little narrow closet next to the stove with a broom and mop and a dust mop in it, and a dustpan and various jars of wax and polish left over from Mom. We found a can of

Butcher's Wax that was almost empty. Nobody would ever open it; nobody had polished the floors since Mom had gone. We wrapped the money up in wax paper like a sandwich, rammed it into the can, jammed the top back on, and put it back in the closet. It'd be safe enough there for a while. Then we sat down at the kitchen table, and I told Sally the whole story, about the kickbacks and everything.

She was pretty impressed that I'd done such a thing. She was scared, but she was impressed. "Weren't you scared?"

"No," I said. "Well, a little. I guess I was sort of scared."

"What'll happen when he finds out?"

"He won't know who to blame. He wouldn't be able to take a chance on blaming anybody. He'll just have to forget about it."

We talked about it for a little while and then we decided to go to bed before Dad came home. I didn't want to talk to him yet; I didn't want to see him. So Sally got undressed and put on her pajamas in the living room, and I snuck into her room so as not to wake up Henry, and I made up my bed on the sofa and started to take my clothes off, too. And that was when I realized that my jackknife wasn't in my pocket where I always carried it: instead, it was lying on the porch floor out at the boat club.

9

I tell you, I had a pretty tough time getting to sleep. The first thing I thought about was putting my clothes on and going back out to the club to get that knife. But I was scared, too. I was afraid that if Dad came home and didn't find me there he'd get all upset and call the police. Besides, I was just scared of going back to that place. But what was I going to do? One thing would be to go out there after school the next day and get the knife, if it was still there. Mr. Slater might not notice it right away. It wasn't too obvious lying on the porch floor. But I didn't like that idea. I didn't want to do anything unusual, just in case he'd already discovered that the money was missing. So that was out. The only thing to do was to wait until I went out as usual on Saturday. The knife might even still be there. But even if he'd found it, he wouldn't necessarily think it was mine. Of course he'd seen me use it before. I'd used the bottle-opener blade a few times when somebody had gone off with the bar bottle opener, and once I'd lent it to him to use the screwdriver blade when he'd wanted to tighten a screw on the cooler-door hinge. But it was just an ordinary knife with a black horn handle. Practically everybody had the same kind. Why would he think it was mine? And anyway, I could easily say that I'd left the knife there last weekend. I could say I was using it to scrape up some chewing gum from the porch floor when I was sweeping up and forgot to pick it up.

I lay there thinking about that. Maybe it would be a smart thing when I got out there Saturday morning to go right up to him and ask him if he'd seen my jackknife, I'd lost it last weekend. But I decided not; it seemed pretty risky to bring up the jackknife at all. The best thing to do, if he asked me about it, was to say it wasn't mine at all. In fact, I suddenly realized, the smart thing to do would be to get another jackknife so if Mr. Slater said anything about it I could show him one.

With all of this going around in my head it was pretty tough getting to sleep. I'd doze off a little and just as I was starting to get into a dream I'd jerk awake, with the jackknife and the money and Mr. Slater going around in my head. I'd try to think about something else, like the Red Sox batting averages, and after a bit I'd doze off; and then I'd jerk awake, this time thinking about how I was going to act when I walked into the clubhouse on Saturday. Would I be able to act natural? Would Mr. Slater have found out that the money was gone by then? These thoughts would go around and around, and

I'd try the Red Sox again, and doze off, and jerk awake. Finally I decided I'd better have a daydream. I tried to pick out out. I thought about having a baseball daydream, and then I thought about having a millionaire daydream. They were both pretty good; I couldn't decide which. And then suddenly I got an idea which combined both of them:

I'm nineteen years old and I'm coming up along Main Street toward our house dressed up in a nice suit and carrying a suitcase. I don't live here anymore, but Dad is still living here, and so are Sal and Henry. Sal is a senior in high school, and Henry is in the eighth grade. Dad is still shuffling for a living and refusing to get a day job, and they're still just as poor as ever. It's October, about six o'clock at night. They're not expecting me. The sun is about down and the air is kind of crisp. As I come along Main Street a few people sort of glance around at me, but nobody speaks to me. I come to our alley and turn down it. I get to our door and swing it open. Sally is standing at the stove, cooking franks and beans. Dad is sitting in the rocker reading his Saturday Evening Post. *Henry is setting the table. I stand in the door. They look up at me, and suddenly they're all tumbling around me, hugging me and babbling. I stride into the room and put my suitcase down. Dad says, "We've read all about you in the newspapers, son. We're very proud of you." Henry says, "They played the last game of the world series on the radio at school. Everybody came to the auditorium to hear it. When you hit those four home runs the kids just went crazy." I say, "I*

*got lucky." Sally says, "Everybody will be wild
to see you. Everybody wants your autograph.
They're planning to have a day for you." I say,
"That's great." Then I put my suitcase up on the
table and open it up. Lying there is a huge pile
of hundred dollar bills. It's my world series
money. Casually I fling about a thousand dollars
on the kitchen table. I say, "Here, Dad, find the
kids a better place to live." I reach out a hundred
more. "Sal, go buy yourself a horse." I give her
another hundred. "May as well get yourself a
riding outfit, too." Then I put my arm around
Henry. I say, "I'd get you a horse, too, Henry,
but I bet you'd rather have a two-wheeler. We'll
go down to the store tomorrow."*

Finally I went to sleep. I guess I was pretty tired,
because I didn't even wake up when Dad came in.

Dad slept late in the morning. I figured he had a
bad hangover. Usually he doesn't drink more than
two or three beers when he goes down to the
Colonial. He isn't really that much of a drinker; he's
more of a talker, and he likes to be around with a lot
of people gabbing. Especially since Mom left, there's
nobody for him to talk to around here. But being all
bothered and stirred up the way he was last night, I
figured he was drinking whiskey, which would give
him a hangover. I was just as glad. I still didn't
want to talk to him yet.

Sally and I got Henry off to school, but we didn't
dare move the money into Sally's room, because we
were afraid Dad might suddenly get up and see us
doing it. "It'll be all right in the Butcher's Wax for
now," I said.

"We can move it after school," Sally said. "Henry will probably be outside playing."

So we went to school. I was still feeling sort of shaky. I mean it was a big thing to have three hundred dollars. You could do a lot with it. You could buy a car — not a brand-new one, but a good used one a couple of years old for three hundred bucks. You could go to Europe on the *Queen Mary* for that much money and have a fine tour. I knew, because I'd seen ads for it in some magazine. Oh, you could do a lot with three hundred dollars.

I didn't feel much like playing ball with Charlie after school. That money just kept looming up in my mind, making it hard for me to concentrate on fielding grounders. But I wanted everything to be normal, so I made myself play until five-thirty, when I told Charlie I had to check up on the baby and left.

Dad was sitting in the kitchen reading the *Saturday Evening Post* and smoking a cigarette.

"Hi," I said. I didn't really feel like being friendly to him; I was just being polite.

"Hi, Jack," he said. He looked at me. "I gave you kind of a shiner, didn't I?"

"I guess so," I said. I didn't much want to talk to him, but I didn't want to just walk away or start a fight.

"I never did hit you before, did I? I never spanked you guys once."

"I guess not," I said.

He rubbed his hands over his eyes. "I wish you weren't such a worrywart, Jack. I wish you'd let me do the worrying. You're just a kid."

I wanted to tell him that if I didn't do the worrying nobody would, but I didn't. "I'm fourteen," I said.

"You'll have plenty of things to worry about when you're older. These are the best years of your life. You ought to try to make the best of them. Have some fun. Don't let things get you down. That's always been my rule — look on the bright side. You only live once."

If he started to sing "Happy Days Are Here Again," I knew I'd completely blow up. "We always seem to be so broke all the time," I said.

"Times are hard," he said. "They'll pick up eventually."

I sure didn't want to bring up about money, but I had to find out what we owed, so I could pay the most important bills, and I knew I had to bring up the subject when the other kids weren't around. I got up my courage. "Listen, Dad, I don't want to keep harping on it, but do we owe a lot of money? I mean the gas bill and the electric?"

"For God's sake, Jack, let's stop talking about it before we have another fight."

"Dad," I said, "I have some money."

"Jack, that's thoughtful of you, but five or ten dollars isn't going to make much difference."

He would never believe it if I told him I had three hundred dollars. "Dad, I have fifty dollars."

"Fifty dollars? Where did you get that much?"

"I saved it."

He stared at me. "How the hell did you save fifty dollars out of your salary?" I could see that he was figuring it up in his mind. I hadn't thought he'd do that.

"I had some saved already."

"I don't see how you could have done it."

"I've been washing people's cars," I said. "They give me fifty cents each."

"Fifty cents for a car wash? That's pretty steep."

"I know it is, but they're all rich, and they don't know how much things cost."

He thought about it. "It still doesn't add up."

"Well, I have the money."

He stared at me hard. "Jack, you haven't been stealing, have you?"

"Of course not," I said. "That isn't a fair thing to say."

"Okay," he said. "I don't think you'd steal."

"It's not fair to make accusations like that," I said.

"All right, I take it back. But I still don't see how you could have saved that much."

I shrugged and tried to calculate quickly in my head. "Well, see, I had fifteen dollars saved up from my other job, and I usually make around two dollars a weekend washing cars. That's another fifteen. And then I earned five dollars tending bar for Mr. Waterman. And the rest I just saved."

"How come Mr. Slater lets you wash cars when you're supposed to be working?"

"I do it when things are slow. He doesn't mind."

He considered it. "I guess so," he said. "That's pretty good going for a kid your age to save up fifty bucks."

"So the thing is, Dad, I could give it toward the back rent."

He shook his head. "No," he said. "You keep it. You'll need it some day."

"I don't need it," I said. "I'll lend it to the family. You can pay me back when the country club re-opens."

"No, Jack, you keep it. I know you want to help,

160

but fifty dollars isn't going to make much difference one way or another in the long run."

"It would keep us from being evicted."

"Jack, no," he said. "Let's not get into that again. I'll do something about that. I'm going to New York again pretty soon and see if I can pick up some more work. I know I didn't get anything last time, but that's the luck of the draw. You win some and you lose some. I'm due to hit pay dirt. I'm building up my connections. No reason why I can't grab off three or four gigs over a weekend, make fifty, seventy, maybe even a hundred bucks. If I can do that a couple of times a month, we'll be in clover."

"But, Dad — " I said.

"Don't you worry about it, Jack," he said. "I'll take care of it."

There wasn't any point in arguing about it anymore. I couldn't make him take the money if he didn't want to. What a crazy thing it was. Here I'd taken this huge risk of stealing all that money just so we could pay up some of the bills and see that the family stayed together, and Dad wouldn't take it. It was just nuts. It made me mad. It wasn't fair.

Dad went down to New York on Thursday to look for work. He still had a long time to go before he could get his union card, but the union delegates didn't come around checking very much — there were hundreds of jobs going on around New York all the time and the delegates could only check on a few of them. He took the afternoon train down. Sally made him a sandwich. He said he'd call us in a day or two. He didn't say anything about what we were supposed to do if the rent man began to evict us.

"We'll just pay him," I told Sally.

"What'll Dad say when he finds out?"

"I guess he'll be sore, but I don't think he'll be too sore. I wish we could find out what else we owe. I mean what about the iceman and the electricity bill and the gas bill?"

"We'll just have to wait until they come around to shut us off," she said.

I didn't sleep too well that night, either. That money kept going around in my head; I couldn't get it out of my mind. I'd concentrate on baseball — I'd name all the catchers I could think of who hit left-handed or try to think of how many first basemen ever led their league in hitting. That would work pretty well and I'd doze off, and then the money would pop into my head and scare me awake. I tell you, I was beginning to hate that money.

On Friday I told Charlie I couldn't practice. "Dad went down to New York and I have to look after the baby."

"He'll be all right by himself," Charlie said.

"I have to," I said.

I went home quickly. Sally wasn't there yet, but Henry was. He was sitting at the kitchen table eating a piece of bread and butter with sugar on it. "You're not supposed to be eating all that sugar," I said. "It's bad for your teeth."

"There wasn't anything else to eat," he said.

"You could have had just plain bread and butter."

"That's yicky," he said.

"I don't care, no more sugar on your bread. Now finish that up and go outside and play."

"Why do I have to go outside?"

"Because it's too nice a day to stay inside," I said. I didn't know if he'd go for all these excuses.

"That's no reason," he said. "You have to give me a good reason."

"No, I don't," I said. "You have to do what I say."

"You're not my boss," he said.

"Yes, I am," I said. "When Dad's gone, I'm your boss."

"Well, anyway, you have to give me a good reason."

"Damn it, Henry, stop arguing with me. Now finish that up and go outside."

"Give me one good reason."

I smacked my fist down on the metal tabletop, making it boom. "I'll give you a good reason on your fanny if you don't get going," I shouted.

He jumped up and crammed the rest of his bread into his mouth. "You don't have to shout," he said, "I'm going."

He got his rubber ball and went outside. The minute he was gone I whipped over to the broom closet, knelt down on the floor, and opened up the Butcher's Wax can. I half expected that the money would be gone, but it wasn't — it was all there. Quickly I counted out seventy-five dollars and shoved it into my pocket. I would liked to have given the rent man everything we owed him, but I didn't dare. Dad would sure want to know where I'd got a hundred and twenty-five dollars from. Seventy-five was as far as I dared to stretch it. I closed the can and put it back. Then I got the *Saturday Evening Post* Dad had left and sat there at the kitchen table, waiting.

The rent man showed up at four o'clock. "I hope your old man's home," he said.

"No," I said. "He isn't home. But he left some

163

money for the rent." I took the seventy-five dollars out of my pocket and counted it out for him. He was pretty surprised to see it. It made me feel pretty good to pay him off. "Do I get a receipt or something?" I asked.

He took out a pad and began filling in the receipt. "That still leaves twenty-five dollars owing," he said, "and another twenty-five at the end of the month."

"Dad said to tell you he'll have it pretty soon. He's getting some good jobs down in New York. He's planning to catch up on the bills." It sounded so real when I put it that way that I almost believed it myself — believed that Dad really was going to get a lot of work down in New York and we'd have money coming in and be able to get a better place to live and buy hamburgers or even steak sometimes and ice cream for dessert instead of canned peaches. But then the man handed me the receipt and I stopped dreaming.

I still felt pretty good when Sally came home and I told her about it, but the feeling died down after a while. I was getting more and more worried about Mr. Slater, too. I kept thinking about calling up Saturday morning and telling him I was sick. But I was afraid to do that, because if Mr. Slater had already found out that the money was missing he'd sure be suspicious if I didn't come to work.

Dad came back Friday night just before supper. He fixed himself a bologna sandwich and ate in a hurry. "I have a gig with Dave," he said. "I'm supposed to meet him down at the Colonial in five minutes."

"Did you get any jobs?" Sally said.

"Things were kind of slow," he said. "You kids be good. I'll be back around twelve-thirty."

Sally and I cooked buttered spaghetti for supper. "We've got to eat more than spaghetti," I said. "There aren't enough vitamins in spaghetti."

"What do you expect me to do?" she said.

"Don't we have anything else?"

"We're having canned pears for dessert."

"Yicky," Henry said. It was his new word.

"I have fifty cents on me," I said. "I'll go out and get a can of peas."

"Yicky," Henry said.

"Stop saying everything is yicky," Sally said.

"Shut up, Henry," I said, "or I'll give you a bruise." I went out and got a can of peas and some brown bread, and we ate them with the spaghetti. It was pretty good. Over supper Sally and I made up a game — what would you do if you had three hundred dollars and you had to spend it on yourself and couldn't save it. My first ideas was that I'd take a trip to Europe on the *Queen Mary* and go on a tour. But then I decided I'd rather spend it by going to all the Red Sox home games and sit in a box seat right behind home plate. I figured it would be a good investment to watch big-league pitching, although I didn't tell Sally and Henry that.

Henry said he would buy a two-wheeler.

"Henry, you could buy about fifty two-wheelers with that much money," I said.

"Oh," he said. "Well, I'd buy an airplane, then."

"That's too much," Sally said. "Airplanes cost more than that."

He looked cross. "Well what could I buy?"

"How about a motorboat?" I said. "You could buy a motorboat for three hundred dollars." I knew what motorboats cost from listening to people talk about them at the boat club.

"I don't want a motorboat," he said.

"Well some kind of a boat," I said. "A sailboat."

"Why are you making him have a boat?" Sally said. "He doesn't want a boat. Let him choose whatever he wants."

"Yeah," Henry said. "I can choose whatever I want."

"All right, you think about it," I said. "What are you going to pick, Sal?"

"A horse," she said.

"I knew you were going to say that," I said. "How do you know what a horse costs?"

"I looked in the ads. I could get a horse for fifty dollars. Then I'd get a whole riding costume — jodhpurs and a little hat and a fancy English saddle because that's more fashionable than western saddles; and I'd ride and ride and take lessons and everything and go into horse shows and win a lot of prizes."

"I know what I want," Henry said suddenly.

"What?" we said.

"A cow," he said.

Sally and I began to laugh.

"What's so funny?" he said. "Then we'd always have lots of milk."

We kidded Henry about his cow until he started to get sore, and then we soothed him down and finished dinner, and Henry, and I washed the dishes because Sal had cooked. Then we put Henry to bed and Sally went to do her homework. I decided I'd do my homework for once and got out my math book; but the minute I was by myself, my whole trouble about the money and Mr. Slater popped back into my mind. We still hadn't moved the money into Sally's room. Sally hadn't brought up about moving it,

166

and I guessed she was probably scared of having it in her bureau. It seemed all right there in the Butcher's Wax can, so I decided to leave it where it was.

I worked away at my homework for a little while, but what with all my worries I didn't get much done, so I got out the victrola and listened to records for awhile — mostly swing records, like Berrigan's "I Can't Get Started." After that I sat up until eleven-thirty finishing the *Saturday Evening Post*. Then I went to bed. I was still having trouble getting to sleep. I'd get shuffled down and about ready to doze off, when suddenly I'd jerk awake and lie there feeling scared. It was like an automatic machine that you can't stop. Just as soon as I'd get myself lowered down into sleep, my troubles would come up and scare me awake. It was like two cement buckets on a pulley; if you let one down the other one has to come up whether you like it or not.

So I was only half asleep when Dad came home. Usually I didn't wake up when he came in — after all those years I was just used to it. But being all messed up with the worries, I wasn't really asleep and I heard him shut the door. He was talking to somebody. I figured it was Dave Johnson. Some-times if Dave drove him home from a gig, they'd pick up a couple of quarts of beer on the way home and come in and play records low and drink the beer. Dave was really interested in jazz. His favorite was Frankie Trumbauer, a saxophone player who made a lot of records with the great Bix Beider-becke. Usually they would get out the Box records when Dave was there. And sure enough, in about five minutes Dad tiptoed into the living room, fum-bled around in the record cabinet in the dark so as not to wake me up, got some records, and went back into the kitchen. They played the records soft. I didn't mind. It relieved my troubles to lie there in the dark, listening to the music. So I sort of lay there drowsing; and then suddenly I realized that they weren't playing records anymore; they were talking in a slow, serious way.

"What would you do?" Dad said. "My wife's in the bughouse, I'm left with three kids on my hands and no money."

"I thought her folks were well off," Dave said.

"They've got enough," Dad said. "They're just not parting with it. They blame me for her breakdown."

"It's pretty rough," Dave said.

"It sure is," Dad said. "I'm really up against it. I wanted to keep things going here for the kids, but I just don't know how I can do it. God knows, I've tried. I did the best I could. I really wanted to keep a home for them here. I put everything I had into it, honest I did, Dave."

"You can't blame yourself for the depression," Dave said.

"I really tried my best. I kept trying to look on the bright side, but it isn't enough."

"If you got a couple of good gigs. . . ."

"No, it's no good, Dave. It's over. I'm way behind on the rent, they're about to cut off the electricity, I've got bills all over town. There's no way out of it."

"What about the kids?"

"I really tried, Dave. I did the best I could."

"Where will the kids go?" Dave said.

"I've been dickering with their grandparents down in New Orleans. They're willing to take Sally. They say the boys would be too rough for them at their age. They're used to having things genteel."

168

"That's pretty rotten of them. You'd think they'd want to help out their own flesh and blood."

"They don't think I'm their flesh and blood," Dad said.

"But the kids are. You'd think they'd be happy to take them for a while."

"Not a chance," Dad said. "I've been over it with them. They'll have Sally but not the boys." Dad let out a long sigh. "It's all money, Dave," he said. "If I had the dough I'd get out of this dump and bring in a housekeeper to look after them. Then it'd be all right. But I haven't got any dough."

"What'll you do with them?"

"Well, Jack's no problem. Hell, the kid saved fifty dollars washing cars out there at the boat club. He's only got three more years of school left. I could probably fix it up for him to stay with some family in town. Maybe with Eddie Franks — you know Eddie? His kid's a pal of Jack's. I'd like to see him go to college, but God knows that isn't likely."

"What about the baby?"

"My wife's brother out in Chicago said he would take him. They haven't got any kids of their own; I guess they'd be glad to have him. Edgar's in insurance. He makes a good buck — nothing fantastic, but enough. When the old folks kick off, he's due for some more, too."

"Well, at least the kids will be taken care of. Maybe it's better that way."

"Dave, I don't want to do it," Dad said. "I don't want to scatter them all over the country. But it seems like I haven't got any choice."

"Well, you know what the answer is, Warren," Dave said.

"I know. The mill."

169

"Jobs come up," Dave said. "I could fix something up for you."

They were silent. Then Dad said, "I'll tell you what the thing really is, Dave. Here I am thirty-seven years old, and I've got nothing to show for it. No money in the bank, no home, just an unknown trombone player stuck away in some hick town."

"There's no reason to feel bad about it, Warren. The depression wasn't your fault."

"What difference does it make? Look at all those guys with the swing bands; there isn't any depression on for them. Look at Dorsey, he's going great guns. Look at Jack Jenney, he can work anywhere he wants. Look at Pee Wee Hunt, he's making a pile of dough with Casa Loma. Hell, ten years ago those guys were nobody; they weren't doing as good as I was."

"They got lucky, Warren," Dave said.

"Naw, it wasn't luck; they were in New York, that's what it was," Dad said. "They weren't stuck way up here in Stevenstown. If I'd have gone with Whiteman when I could have, I'd be on top."

"There's a lot of luck in it," Dave said.

"You have to be in the right place at the right time," Dad said. "This is my last go-round, Dave. In a few years I'm going to be too old. Those kids out in front of the bandstand, they don't want to look up and see some gray-haired old guy playing trombone; they want to see somebody young. Look at Goodman, how old is he? He's still in his twenties, isn't he?"

"Around thirty," Dave said.

"There you are," Dad said. "I have to do it now."

"What do you figure you'll do?" Dave said.

"I'm going down to New York. As soon as I get the kids settled, I'll get out of this hick town, get myself a little place down in New York, and see what I can do. I should have done it years ago. I should never have been talked into staying up here all these years. Sure, it was nice for the kids to grow up in a place like this, but look what it did to me. It wouldn't have hurt them to grow up in New York."

"You figure you can cut it down there?" Dave said.

"Sure I can. Sooner or later a spot for a good trombone player will open up. Once they see I can cut anything they throw at me, the jobs will open up. When I get hooked up with a swing outfit I'll be able to build up my name. Get some solo spots, maybe even do a little arranging. After I've got the name, I'll see about putting together a band of my own. All I need is some backing, and I figure that once I've got the name I can get the dough."

"I don't think it'll be that easy," Dave said.

There was the thump of Dad banging his fist down on the enamel table. "I've got to do it, Dave," he said. "I've got to do it now before it's too late."

"Shhh," Dave said, "you'll wake up your kids."

They lowered their voices and I couldn't hear them anymore. So there it was. Dad had no idea of trying to keep us together and he never had. To him the whole thing was to make it in the big time. For the first time I could see it all pretty clear. As long as Mom had been okay, she'd made him stay in Stevenstown. I guess she just kept talking him into it all the time. But now she was gone, and all he could think about was getting down to New York. The only reason why he hadn't broken up the family before was because of his usual way of worrying about things tomorrow. And I could see clear enough that if he'd been a more organized person, he'd have got rid of us and gone down to New York months before.

I thought about it. What right had he to put himself first? What right had he to split up the family just so he could go down to the big time? What right had he to shove us off on our relatives so he could try to make himself into a star? I lay there fuming about it, but in my head I knew there was no use fuming. He was going to end up doing what he wanted to do.

So the whole thing hadn't been any use, right from the beginning. It hadn't been any use for me to try to save money, or pay the rent, or least of all to steal all that money from Mr. Slater. It had just been stupid, just some sort of dumb idea that couldn't ever work. Sooner or later — when he got around to it — he'd send Henry off to Chicago and Sally off to New Orleans and dump me on the Frankses if he could. And knowing him, I could tell exactly how it would happen. He'd go drifting along the way he always did until we got up to a crisis — we got evicted or the bills all got too big to pay or something. Then in about two days we'd pack up everything and he'd put Sal on the train for New Orleans, take Henry out to Chicago, and send me over to the Frankses'. That was going to be pretty embarrassing, because Dad would promise to send the Frankses money for my room and board, and of course half the time he wouldn't send it.

Boy, what a useless thing it was to rob that money from Mr. Slater. All that trouble and worry for nothing. Here I'd taken a chance on going to jail to keep the family from splitting up; and there hadn't been any hope of it all along.

Suddenly I decided I was going to put the money back. The whole thing was useless. Why should I suffer over it? Why should I go on worrying about it and not being able to sleep night after night? It wasn't worth it anymore. It would be better to put it back and forget about it. Some of it was missing, that was true. Mr. Slater would be pretty puzzled about that when he counted it. But I didn't care about that as long as it was off my neck. So that was decided. All at once I felt a lot better and rolled over and went to sleep. I didn't wake up when Dave Johnson left and Dad went to bed.

10

O n Thursday after school I had gone down to
Pete's Smoke Shop and bought a jackknife.
It was just the same regular kind with a
black bone handle, like everybody had.
Then I went out to practice with Charlie. When I
got home at six o'clock I went out back behind the
apartment, dropped the knife down onto the cement,
put my foot on it, and scuffed the knife back and
forth along the ground. When I'd got it scuffed up
pretty well, I got a handful of ashes out of the ash
can and rubbed them over it. It was a shame to scuff
up a new knife like that, but I had to. It looked
pretty old.

When I got up Saturday morning the sun was shining into the kitchen window. It was going to be a
nice day. I was just as glad. We would be pretty busy
and I wouldn't have to talk to Mr. Slater very much.
I drank a cup of coffee. Then I got the can of Butcher's Wax out of the closet and took the money out of

174

it. I unwrapped the bills, peeled off ten to pay myself back for Sally's outfit, and another ten so I could give Henry and Sally each five bucks when they got shipped off to relatives. That left two hundred and twenty dollars. I figured the heck with it; Mr. Slater had stolen the money from the boat club, anyway. I put the two tens into my flat fifties money box and shoved the rest of it into my back pocket. Then I went outside and hitched out to the boat club. I was pretty scared when I walked into the clubhouse. I was worried that when I first saw Mr. Slater I wouldn't be able to act normal. I'd stutter or look scared or embarrassed or something. But it was okay. He was in his office when I came in. I said, "Good morning, Mr. Slater," the way I usually did, and he nodded and I got out the broom and began to sweep. The first thing I did was to sweep my way out onto the porch and see if my jackknife was still there. It wasn't; it was gone. But there was no telling what that meant. Maybe Mr. Slater found it; but it was just as likely that some kid picked it up and kept it, too.

By nine o'clock it was getting hot, and there were a pretty fair number of people out on the dock fooling around with their boats and a lot of kids running around the clubhouse heaving chair pillows at each other and asking for soda pop. I didn't really get my cleaning finished until they went off to their sailing class, and by then grown-ups were coming in asking for beers. We were already serving before we got the bar properly set up, and we had to keep the bar open until nearly three. A lot of people had brought picnics and kept coming in and asking for drinks and sodas and ice for their lunches. Mr. Slater didn't say much to me, just stuff like, "Fill the ice well as soon

175

as you 'ave a chonce, Jack," or "Let's get some more beer in the cooler." Then, by the time I got the bar cleaned up and the clubhouse swept and had a quick run around the porch and dock to pick up empty bottles and papers it was time to set up the bar again for the evening rush. It was a busy day; and I didn't even get much chance to think about how I was going to return the money until I went outside to do the empties. I went over it in my mind. What I figured I'd do was to make sure one of the porch windows was unlocked. There was always a chance that Mr. Slater would go around the windows and lock them, but I knew I could unlock it again if I had to. Then, when we closed up for the evening I'd go down the drive as usual, but instead of going out through the gate I'd duck off into the pines and hide there until Mr. Slater drove out. After that it would only take me about five minutes to get into the clubhouse and put the money back into the sleeping bag. So that was the plan. The only thing I didn't know was whether Mr. Slater had already discovered that the money was gone. If he hadn't, he might go on shoving fresh money into the sleeping bag all summer without ever knowing anything was missing.

Finally it got dark and the bar crowd thinned out and began to go home. While Mr. Slater was finishing up the last customer, I began cleaning the bar — washing up the glasses and putting them away, taking the garbage out, filling the cooler with beer and soda pop for the morning. By the time I'd got this done the last customer was leaving. Mr. Slater emptied out the cash register and took the money over to his office to count it. I gave the bar a last swab, and then I picked up the broom, walked across the clubhouse to the front door, and went out onto the porch. I gave it a quick sweep, and then I came back in again. As I came through the door I glanced at Mr. Slater's office. He was crouched down in front of the safe putting the money away. All I could see of him was part of his back. I stepped over to the nearest window and leaned on it, and as if I was just looking out at the lake. My body was between the window and Mr. Slater. I swiveled open the catch, went across the club room and put the broom away. Then I crossed to Mr. Slater's office and stood by the door. "I guess that's got it," I said. "Is it okay if I take off?"

Mr. Slater was still crouched in front of the safe. "'ang on 'arf a mo', Jack. I want to talk to you about something."

That worried me a little. I figured he probably wanted to talk to me about working there full time in the summer, but it certainly wasn't the night I wanted to have a serious talk with him. "Okay," I said. I went over by the bar and stood there, waiting. Finally he was finished with the safe and stood up. "Come on in, Jack." I walked across to his office, hoping that I was acting normal. I sure wished I didn't have his two hundred and twenty dollars in my back pocket. I reached back and touched it, just to make sure it wasn't sticking up.

He wasn't sitting behind his desk but was in front of it, leaning on it. "Shut the door," he said.

I shut the door. He had one hand in his pocket, and casually he brought it up and held it out toward me, palm up, with the fist closed. Then he opened his fist. My jackknife was lying in his hand. "I think you left this 'ere the other night," he said.

I stared at it for a minute. Then I shook my head slowly. "It isn't mine, Mr. Slater." I reached into my

177

pocket and took out the new knife I'd scuffed up. "See," I said. "Here's mine." I held it out.

He grabbed it out of my hand and looked at the two together. "Hmmmph," he said under his breath. Then he put the old knife down on the desk and carefully opened up the big blade on the new knife. Right away I knew I'd made a mistake. The big blade was shiny and sharp. There wasn't a mark on it — no scratches, no stains, no bits of rust. There weren't even those lines you get near the edges when you sharpen it. What a dope I'd been. I'd carefully scuffed up the outside, and I'd forgotten about the blades completely.

"Pretty new, in't it?" Mr. Slater said.

"I got it last year," I said. "I don't use it much." I was blushing from lying and feeling pretty scared.

He looked it over, and then he opened the other blades — the screwdriver, the leather punch, and the little blade. They were all bright and gleaming, too. "Funny 'ow it's all roughed up on the outside, but bright and shiny inside."

"I don't use it much," I said. "Nobody ever uses the leather punch."

He put the knife down on the desk beside the other one. Then suddenly his hand shot out and grabbed hold of my wrist, clutching it tightly as he could.

"Hey," I said.

"Where is it?" he sort of hissed.

I was pretty scared. "What?" I kind of whispered.

"You know bloody well what. Where is it?"

I didn't say anything, but stared at him, and he stared back. He started to squeeze my wrist. "Where is it? Or 'ave you spent it already, you bloody little thief?"

I didn't know whether to admit I had the money, or what to do. I knew there wasn't much chance he would call the cops about it, but still, it's scary to have people know you're a thief. "Let go of my wrist," I said.

"Oh no, you bloody thief. You tell me where the money is 'id first."

"It isn't hidden," I said. He was hurting my wrist and I was beginning to get mad — scared, too, but getting more mad than scared. Why was it me who was in all this trouble, when I'd only been trying to help? I blurted out, "If you want to know where the money is, I'll tell you," I said.

He loosened up his hand on my wrist. "Where?"

"Let go of my wrist, first," I said.

"Oh, no, sonny boy — not and 'ave you make a break for it."

I stared at him. "Let go first," I said.

He thought about it, and then he let go, but he stood with his hands in front of him ready to make a grab for me if I started to run. I rubbed my wrist where he'd hurt it, and then I reached into my back pocket, pulled out the money, and threw it on his desk next to the jackknives. "I was bringing it back," I said. "Some of it's missing. I used it to pay the rent so we wouldn't get evicted."

He snatched it up from the desk and counted it. "That's a bloody lie," he said. "Where's the rest of it?"

"I don't care if you believe me," I said. "It's the truth." I was still nervous, but I was good and sore, too. What right did he have to question me when he'd stolen the money himself?

He grabbed my wrist again and stared into my eyes. "Where's the rest of the money, Jack?"

"God damn it, let go of my wrist."

"Don't you rise your voice with me, sonny," he said.

"Let go of it," I shouted.

"Sonny boy," he said, "you'll be lucky if you don't end up in jail. What did you do with the money?"

"Let go of my wrist," I shouted. "I know you're taking kickbacks."

For a fraction of a second he looked startled. Then he hissed out, "That's a lie."

"The hell it is," I said. "I heard you. I know you're taking kickbacks from Eddie and a lot of other ones, too."

"You rotten little bahstid," he said between his teeth. "You're a filthy little spy. I ought to beat you within an inch of your life."

"You wouldn't dare," I said. "You'd have to kill me first, or I'll spill it to Mr. Waterman." I was pretty much in a rage and I didn't care what I said anymore. The only thing that worried me was that I might start to cry, too; I sure didn't want to do that in front of Mr. Slater.

"You little bahstid," he said.

"And I know you're cheating on the boat club books, too." I wasn't sure of that, but I figured it was true and anyway, raging the way I was, I didn't care what I said.

He stared at me and then he let go of my wrist. He folded his arms across his chest. Then he lit a cigarette. "All roight, Jack," he said. "Let's both calm down a bit. No good losing our tempers, is there?"

I didn't say anything, just went on staring at him. My fists were clenched down by my sides, and the tears were coming up behind my eyes.

"Let's see if we can work this out," he said. "You say you've spent the rest of the money."

"I paid the rent," I said. "That's what I took it for, to pay the rent."

"All roight," he said. "I'm willing to give you the benefit of the doubt. It's about ninety dollars, isn't it?"

I felt a little calmer, but still wrought up. "ninety-five," I said.

"Fine," he said. "Now Jack, I know you're basically an honest lad, no doubt the temptation was too much, but let's say you've learned a bit of a lesson. No need to get the police in on it. I think I'd be willing to do the generous thing and keep you on 'ere at the club, if we can work out an arrangement for you to pay me back a bit at a toime."

I wasn't much scared of him anymore, just all wrought up. "How could I pay you back out of six dollars week?"

"Oh roight," he said. "Actually, I was planning to ask you to come on full time when school term was over."

I didn't say anything.

"Suppose we fix you a salary of twenty-five a week. If you paid me back fifteen dollars a week out of that, you'd clean it up in six weeks and you'd still end up with a noice bit of cash at the end of the summer."

It was fishy. He wouldn't have had to pay me more than twenty dollars a week. Probably he'd have been able to get somebody for sixteen or seventeen. The whole idea was to give me enough so he could collect his money out of it. What it came down to was stealing it from the boat club. "I couldn't pay

181

back that much," I said. "Dad's hardly working at all, we'd need the money."

He shrugged. "Roighty-oh. I'm not a 'ard man, Jack. Pay me ten a week, and we'll still be even before the summer's over."

And what would happen then? Would he fire me as soon as he'd got his money back? Would he go on taking the ten dollars out? It was all rotten. It would make me into his partner; it would make me into a person just like him. "I'm not going to pay you anything," I said. "I'm not going to pay the money back at all." Suddenly the tears began to run down my face, and I was shouting, "I'm not going to pay you back a God-damned cent." I turned and ran out of the clubhouse and raced down the driveway. And all the way along it kept going through my head, why was it always up to me to take care of everybody? Why was it up to me to see that everything went right and everybody had the things they needed? Why was it up to me?

Down toward the end of the summer I happened to be hitchhiking out to the Watermans' place, where I'd got part-time work helping around on the grounds. I never did know what Mr. Slater had told people about why I wasn't working there anymore, but I figured he was afraid to say anything bad about me; anyway, when I asked Mr. Waterman for a job, he gave me one. I went out there two days a week and sometimes helped out at parties. Anyway this one day I was going out there and Dave Johnson drove by and picked me up.

"Where are you going, Jack?" I told him and he

182

said he was going near there and would drop me at the Watermans'.

"Thanks," I said.

"What do you hear from Sally and the baby?" he asked.

"I don't hear much from Henry," I said. "He's pretty little to write letters. He doesn't answer my letters much. I try to write him every couple of weeks, although I guess I miss sometimes."

"And Sally?"

"She's kind of homesick. She writes a lot."

He didn't say anything about that. Then he said, "What's the word from your father?"

"He calls up about once a week," I said. "Or he sends me a postcard if he's on the road. He says things are going okay. I guess he's getting a fair number of gigs."

"He never writes to me, the stinker," Dave Johnson said. "Just a postcard now and then from someplace like Atlantic City."

"He had a couple of jobs down there," I said. "He says things are building up. Pretty soon the money will be rolling in."

Mr. Johnson laughed. "That's your dad," he said. "Always looking on the bright side. That's all I ever heard when we had the Jolly Lads. Let's look on the bright side. I told him he ought to write a song about it."

That was one thing I'd learned out of it: just looking on the bright side wasn't good enough. If you didn't pay the rent you got evicted, and looking on the bright side didn't help. But I didn't say that. Instead I said, "Mr. Johnson, is Dad really a pretty good musician?"

"Sure," he said. "He's real good."

"I mean like Dorsey or Jack Jenney?"

He laughed. "Nobody's as good as those guys. Those guys are unbelievable."

"So you don't think Dad's good enough to make it?"

"Oh, I didn't say that. He's a good solid pro. He reads like an ace, he's got good tone, good range. He's a pro."

"So he could make it?"

"Jack, there's so much luck in a thing like that. I know a lot of swell musicians who aren't making much and a lot of lousy ones who are doing real well. Your dad could do okay. I mean he ought to be able to work regularly around New York. Maybe go on the road with a name band, something like that. But as far as being a big star or having his own band — that's another story. It's a heck of a complicated business. There's a lot more to it than being a good player. You've got to be tough and aggressive and know how to handle publicity and booking agents and all that stuff. It isn't easy."

I thought about it. "So probably he won't be making a lot of money for a while?"

"Oh, I think he'll begin to make a comfortable income in a couple of years. He has to work out his card and build up his contacts. But your Dad — well, he's not one of these guys like Goodman or Dorsey who has a lot of business sense. To make it like those guys you have to keep your shoulder to the wheel all the time. That isn't exactly your Dad's style. Sure, he loves playing and he'd like to make it big, but let's face it, he doesn't push himself. Now you take me, I'm not ambitious to be a star. Oh, I was once. I wanted to be a great jazz musician. But after the depression came and things got tough, I began to be more realistic. I'm not that good. I'm a solid alto player, not quite as good a musician as your Dad, maybe, but good enough for around Stevenstown. But after things went bad, I decided what was the point in scraping along making half a living for the rest of my life? I'd rather get something more secure and be able to spend some time with my family. Don't get me wrong, I like to play. It suits me to work a couple of nights a week, if I can — play a little, make a few bucks, have a couple of drinks with the boys. But not full time."

"So you think Dad should have got a day job and stayed with the family?"

"I didn't say that, Jack. That's my way. It isn't his. He just isn't the steady, reliable type. He tried to stick it out with you kids, but it just wasn't in him. He's not much of a family man, if you want to know the truth. He never should have got married. There's no point in trying to change him. You just can't do it. I gave up on the idea years ago when we had the Jolly Lads."

We got to the Watermans', and I got out. "You still living at the Frankses'?"

"Yes," I said.

"Going all right?"

"It's all right — when Dad remembers to send the dough."

"Well, give him my best next time he calls. And tell him to write me a real letter once in awhile, the stinker." He waved, and drove off. And I guessed he was right. There was no point in trying to change Dad. You'd never be able to do it.

About the Author

James Lincoln Collier lives in New York City. He is the father of two sons, Geoffrey and Andrew. Mr. Collier is a musician who has played the trombone professionally and has sat in at jam sessions from San Francisco to Leningrad. With his brother Christopher Collier, he is the coauthor of the Newbery Honor Book, *My Brother Sam Is Dead*, which is available in a Scholastic Paperback edition. He has also written many other highly praised books for children and teenagers.